DAVID ARCHER

A SAM AND INDIE NOVEL

MOVING ON

MOVING
ON

Published by Lone Stone Publishing

ISBN-13: 978-1-987987-98-0 (hardcover)
ISBN-13: 978-1-987987-99-7 (paperback)

First edition

PROLOGUE

Orlando, Florida—home to Disney World, Universal Studios theme parks and more tourist attractions than anybody can attend in a single vacation. It is also one of the hottest party spots in the entire United States, and young people flock to it for its nightclubs, discos and hotspots. There is always something to do, regardless of what time of day or night it might be, and this particular night was no different.

Krista and Lynette had been friends since their very first day at school, nearly twenty years ago. They often called each other sisters, and everyone who knew them was fully aware that if you wanted to hang out with one, you had to put up with the other. Krista's friends weren't always that fond of Lynette, and the same was true of Lynette's friends regarding Krista. The two girls were as different as night and day, and the people they counted as friends often ran into conflict with each other, but somehow the two of them had simply clicked.

"She is just jealous," Lynette said as one of Krista's other friends walked away. The girl had been trying to convince them to go to a new club, but they liked Maxwell's. "She doesn't get why you want to stick with me." Lynette shrugged. "I guess she thinks you'd be better off without me."

"Bump that," Krista said with a grin. "I never have any fun if you don't come along. No, I'm serious, it's like all the guys turn into jerks if you aren't here to be my wingman."

"That's all in your head. Guys are guys, they're always the same." She glanced at the retreating back of the other girl. "You know I wouldn't have gotten upset if you wanted to go hang with her, right?"

"Yeah, I know," Krista said. "But you're more fun. Come on, let's dance."

The two of them giggled and moved onto the dance floor, dancing with each other since none of the guys had recently offered. They knew how to work their routine, however, and it was not long before they were surrounded by several of the young men in the club.

A couple of the guys seemed to get their courage up, and each of the girls leaned back into them when they stepped close. They were dancing in such a way as to drive the boys crazy, and the two girls watched each other, their eyes locked together.

Lynette realized that something was happening first, when she saw Krista's eyes glaze over. Her rhythmic movements suddenly became stilted, and she stumbled backwards into the boy who was dancing close to her, and this was so unlike her that Lynette stopped dancing and reached out to her friend. Krista took her hand and used it to help get her balance, then closed her eyes and shook her head.

"I don't know what's wrong," she said, and her words were slurred, though she'd not had nearly enough to drink this early in the evening. "It's like I'm dizzy, but I'm not dizzy."

She opened her eyes and looked at Lynette, and her friend's face registered shock. As her eyelids opened, blood began to run down her face from under them.

Lynette stared at her for a second, then grabbed her arms and dragged her toward a chair. "Somebody call nine one one," she yelled, and one of the boys took a cell phone out of his pocket. She pushed

Krista into a chair and knelt in front of her. "Honey, I don't know what's going on, but your eyes are bleeding."

Krista blinked and tried to look at her, but the blood was blurring her vision. "Bleeding? Why would they..."

Her words cut off as she coughed, and blood sprayed out of her mouth into Lynette's face. Lynette recoiled instinctively, but then the shock on her face grew deeper as Krista jerked twice and then slumped sideways. She hit the floor with a loud slapping sound, her body completely relaxed, and Lynette went into a panic.

She leaned over her friend, screaming her name, but there was no response. Blood was coming from her mouth, her nose and even out of her ears, but the only sign of life Krista showed was ragged breathing.

"Jesus, look," a voice said behind her, and she glanced back to see a man pointing at Krista. She turned her eyes back to her friend and realized what he was pointing at. Blood was soaking through Krista's white pants, apparently coming from her anus and urethra.

There were scattered screams from the dance floor and the nearby tables, and then the two girls were alone, because a space opened up around them as people tried to get away from the scene. The music stopped and a manager came over to find out what was going on, but then an ambulance arrived and paramedics rushed inside, followed by a number of police officers.

The paramedics pushed Lynette away and got busy. The blood was quickly cleaned away from her face and CPR was administered, but Krista was not responding. After twenty minutes of just trying to get her stabilized, they loaded Krista into the ambulance, and everyone else who was present was loaded into a bus for the ride to the emergency room. At that moment, they were terrified that Krista had fallen victim to some virulent infection, and that many of the others might have been exposed. Because they had been together,

Lynette was ushered into the ambulance beside her nearly lifeless friend.

At the hospital, Krista was rushed into one trauma treatment room and Lynette into another, while everyone else was herded into a larger space for triage. Blood samples were drawn from everyone, and lab technicians were called in. Whatever this was, the entire staff was desperate to identify it quickly before it could become an epidemic.

For more than three hours, Lynette simply sat there on the hospital bed, waiting for someone to tell her what was going on. One of the nurses had stopped in to tell her that Krista was in critical condition, but there was something terrifyingly frantic about the way people were rushing about the emergency room. It did not take a rocket scientist to figure out that they were frightened, and that naturally increased the terror for Lynette, herself.

Even though Krista was still in the very next room, Lynette had been unable to overhear anything the doctors and nurses were talking about in there. On the rare occasion when someone poked their head through the curtain to check on her, they never stayed long enough for her to ask any questions. She was just about to storm out of the room and demand answers when another nurse walked in.

"It's about damn time," she began, but the nurse held up a hand to cut her off.

"Hold on," she said. "My name is Julie, and the first thing I need to tell you is that you don't seem to be infected with anything. We still don't know yet what's going on with your friend, but your blood tests appear to be clean."

A flood of relief struck Lynette, and then she was instantly struck with a sense of guilt and shame. Her friend was in critical condition and possibly dying, and here she was, just happy that she was not likely to die of the same thing that was killing Krista. She forced herself to shake it off and looked at the nurse.

"What do you mean, you don't know what's going on with her?" she asked. "She had blood coming out of her eyes, for God's sake. What can cause that?"

"I will confess that I don't know of anything that can cause bleeding like that," Julie said. "Normally, bleeding from the eyes involves only tiny amounts of blood. It wasn't just the blood vessels in her eyes that burst, it was blood vessels in the tissues behind her eyes. There was enough bleeding for it to force its way around the eyeball and start leaking out past the eyelids." She shook her head. "As far as I know, none of us has ever heard of anything like this before."

"Well, there has to be something," Lynette said. "I saw it, with my own eyes. And then when she coughed, she sprayed a big gob of blood out of her mouth, and then it started coming out of her nose, her ears, even out of her butt! God, it was terrible, but you don't have any idea what it could be?"

The nurse nodded. "Yes, she was hemorrhaging pretty seriously. We found that she has blood in her lungs, and there is bleeding in her brain, and they're still trying to figure out where it all comes from." She gave an expression of sympathy. "The only good news at the moment is that, whatever it is, you don't seem to have been affected. That is something to be thankful for, at least."

Lynette stared at her for a moment, then sagged back onto the bed. "But this just doesn't make any sense," she said. "Krista has always been healthy as a horse. I don't think I've ever even seen her sick, except maybe with a cold."

"Well, that is one of the reasons I'm here," the nurse said. "I'm supposed to ask you some questions, and I need you to understand that these are necessary. Was your friend using any kind of drugs? Whether they were prescribed or just recreational, we need to know."

Lynette narrowed her eyes and scoffed. "Drugs? You've got to be kidding. Her brother got hooked on meth a few years ago and ended up dead, Krista won't even—she wouldn't even smoke pot. No, she would not have been using any kind of drugs."

Julie nodded. "We didn't find any sign of drugs," she said, "but I still had to ask. There is a police detective here who would like to talk to you. Can I send him in now?"

Lynette looked at her for a second, then shrugged. "Sure," she said. "I guess I should've expected that."

Julie reached out and put a hand on her shoulder comfortingly. "Look, I'm sorry about your friend, and I hope we can save her," she said. "But at least you know that you are okay. If this had been some sort of contagious disease, you could've been lying in there next to her." She gave Lynette's shoulder a squeeze and then turned to walk out through the curtain.

A few seconds later, a short, swarthy, dark-haired man poked his head through the curtain with a hand over his eyes, keeping his gaze down at the floor. "Ms. Bennett? I am Detective Edward Garza with Orlando PD."

Lynette waved him inside. "Come on in," she said. "Don't worry, I'm decent, they never made me get undressed."

Garza removed his hand and looked at her, then forced himself to put on a smile as he stepped the rest of the way through the curtain. He closed it behind him and walked over so he was standing just a couple of feet in front of her.

"I'm sorry about your friend," he began. "I'm also sorry that we have to do this right now, but we need to find out as much as we can while everything is still fresh in your mind. Can you tell me exactly what happened? What you saw?" He held up a small recording device.

"Yeah," Lynette said. "We were dancing, me and her and a couple of guys, and everything seemed to be perfectly normal. I mean, we were just having a good time, like we usually do—like we did, anyway. Krista was acting perfectly fine up until the last few seconds, then all of a sudden, she seemed like she was stumbling, getting weak. She kinda fell back into the guy who was dancing with her and I noticed that her eyes looked funny, like they wouldn't focus or something. She reached out and grabbed hold of me and said something was wrong, and when she opened her eyes again, there was blood coming out of them. I got her to sit down and then she coughed up a bunch of blood—right into my face, as a matter of fact—and then she just kinda collapsed. I saw blood coming out of her nose and her ears, and then somebody pointed at the blood soaking through her pants." She shuddered at the memory.

"Did she say anything before this happened, maybe about not feeling good or something?"

Lynette shook her head. "No, she was just her normal, fun-loving self. Everything seemed like it was fine, we were laughing and dancing and having a good time."

Garza nodded. "Okay," he said. "Do you know if she had any enemies?" He looked into her eyes as he asked the question.

Lynette's own eyes suddenly went wide. "Enemies? You gotta be kidding. She was one of the most popular girls in the entire city. Everybody loved her, that's just the way it was." Her eyes suddenly narrowed. "Wait a minute, enemies? Are you saying you think somebody did this to her?"

"I don't really think anything at the moment," Garza said. "I'm simply trying to find out what happened. When someone gets suddenly sick like this and the doctors can't figure out why, it is only standard procedure to ask about enemies."

She looked hard at him for a moment, then shook her head. "I don't know of any enemies," she said. "And I can't imagine any kind of poison or anything that could do this, can you?"

"No," Garza said, "but I'm not a scientist. I have to think it is possible that some kind of poison or drug could do this sort of thing. What about boyfriends? Has she had any bad breakups lately?"

Lynette drew back and looked at him like he was some sort of alien creature. "Krista? She never got serious about anybody. That was probably the only thing about her that was not completely normal—she never got involved with anyone for more than a couple of days at a time. Even the guys she dated now and then, they just took it in stride. It's just the way she was, she always said she wasn't ready to settle down yet."

Garza nodded. "Okay, no problem. What about in the past? Did she have any old boyfriends from the past who might have some sort of grudge?"

"No, never. I mean, she was the kind of girl who made sure she dated every guy in her class in high school, even the nerdy guys and the ones nobody else wanted to go out with. She went out with everybody at least once, because she said everybody had their good points. She didn't care what a guy looked like, or how much he weighed, or what kind of clothes he wore. She just wanted to know everybody."

Garza raised his eyebrows. "Sounds like a pretty great girl," he said. He turned off the recorder and put it back in his pocket. "Listen, Ms. Bennett, we may have more questions for you later. I've already got your address and contact information from the hospital. I'll be in touch if I need to speak with you again, okay?"

"Yeah, that's fine," she said. "And listen, if you find out what happened…"

"Don't worry," Garza said. "I will be certain to call you and let you know."

He turned and left the room, and Julie the nurse came back moments later. She held the clipboard out and handed Lynette a pen.

"I just need to get your signature, and you can go. I wish we could give you more encouraging news tonight."

Lynette scribbled her autograph on the bottom of the form and handed the clipboard back. "Yeah," she said. "You and me both. So, what's going to happen with Krista now?"

"She has been transferred to the ICU," Julie said. "The doctors are doing everything they possibly can, but we're still at a loss about how to treat her. I'm afraid all we can do right now is pray."

Lynette picked up her purse and held it while Julie cut the hospital bracelet off her wrist, then she stepped through the curtain and started toward the doors. She had gone only a few steps when the doors slid open and paramedics came rushing through with someone on a gurney.

She had to step aside to let them by, and the natural instinctive curiosity of all human beings made her look at the face of the person they were wheeling in. There was a plastic oxygen mask over the man's nose and mouth, but her eyes went wide when she saw that it was filled with blood, and that there was blood streaming out of his eyes and nose.

Everyone was rushing around again, the same doctors and nurses who had gathered around Krista flocking toward this new victim. Lynette stared after them for a moment, then turned and hurried out the door before anyone could stop her.

Whatever this was, she had a feeling that it was just beginning.

ONE

Sam Prichard stepped through the sliding glass doors onto the deck with a large mug of coffee in his hand, then leaned on his cane as he walked over to the deck chair and sat down. He kicked his feet up onto a footstool and leaned his cane against the table beside him, then took a big sip from his coffee before setting it on the table. He let his eyes look out over the view before him, watching the surf breaking against the beach.

He glanced at his cane. "You see what you are cheating me out of?" he asked. "Wasn't for you, I'd buy myself a surfboard."

He turned back to watch the ocean and let his thoughts drift back over the last few months. They had been the hardest time of his life, filled with pain and loss that had threatened to destroy him for a while, but the beauty of the scene in front of him had turned out to be an appropriate therapy.

Almost seven months ago, Sam had buried his mother, who had died at the hand of the long-lost twin he had not even known about until he was arrested and charged with being a serial killer. His DNA had come up as a probable match for several murders, but his ensuing investigation had determined that it was actually the DNA of the twin brother that everyone thought had died shortly after they were born. A nurse at the hospital had switched one of the twins with another baby who had passed away suddenly, trying to ease the grief of the mother who had lost her only child. Sam and his friends from Windlass Security had been forced to track the real killer, which had ended in a confrontation between Sam and C.J., his long-lost twin.

C.J. had been holding them at gunpoint: Sam, Indie and both of their mothers. When Kenzie had awakened and come to see what all the noise was about, C.J. had been distracted for just a moment and pointed his gun at her. Sam had lunged at him, trying to protect his daughter, but C.J. had ducked aside and Sam had fallen. In that moment, while C.J. was distracted, Sam's mother Grace had picked up a pistol that had been by her foot and fired, striking C.J. in the chest.

Unfortunately, C.J. had also fired, and the bullet took Grace's life. It was one of the most horrible times of Sam's life, comparable only to when his father had died years earlier. It had taken him a while to get himself back together, but then, only a couple of months later, he had lost two of his dearest friends to another killer. While investigating a cold case involving the murder of a minister twenty-five years earlier, they had uncovered a connection between the preacher and the abduction and murder of several children. In the final confrontation, Jade Miller and Darren Beecher, two of the investigators Sam had worked with for the past couple of years, lost their lives. Sam had been wounded and nearly died himself, and he'd decided that was the last straw.

As soon as he was recovered enough to have visitors, Sam announced his decision. He was retiring, giving up investigations for good. Over the past few years, he and Indie had put away quite a lot of money, and it was not going to be difficult to live comfortably for the rest of their lives.

As soon as he was released from the hospital, Sam called a family council. Kim, Indie's mother, had inherited Grace's house, but she was spending most of her time at their home, so she was included.

"I've been giving this a lot of thought," Sam began. "And I think it's time we make some big changes in our lives."

Indie stared at him. "What kind of changes, Sam?" she asked. He grinned at her when he noticed that she seemed nervous.

"Well, a couple that I think you might like. I don't know about the rest of you, but my hip has been giving me trouble every winter since it got messed up. I am beginning to feel like it might be time to relocate to a warmer climate. How would you all feel about us moving to Florida?"

The only one who did not seem completely shocked was little Bo. At almost a year old, he did not really care a whole lot where he lived as long as Mommy and Daddy and the rest were there to make sure life was good.

"Florida?" Indie asked. "Sam, are you serious?"

Sam grinned and nodded. "I absolutely am," he said. "Look, honey, money is something we don't have to worry about. I am thinking a nice place on the beach might be exactly what we need. Let's get out of Denver—there's too much sadness here for us. Heck, I can't even walk through our living room without feeling like the world is caving in on me."

Indie swallowed hard. "Well, what about Mom?"

Sam turned to his mother-in-law. "Kim? You'd come with us, wouldn't you?"

Kim's eyes were wide. "To Florida? Of course, Sam, but what would I do with the house?"

"Kim, Mom left you the house so that you would have it to do whatever you want to do with. You can keep it if you want, or you can put it up for sale. Considering the neighborhood it's in, I think you could probably get somewhere in the high six figures, and that's without even holding out for a higher offer. Imagine having that kind of money to live on, but you could just stay with us and make it last about forever."

Kim stared at him, but Indie tapped his hand to get his attention. "And we sell our place?" she asked.

"Of course," Sam said. "Look, Carrie is out in Hollywood, neither of us has any other family here, so there's no reason to stay, no reason to come back here. It's time we move on, and just devote some time to our own lives."

Indie looked at him for another moment, then turned to look at her daughter. "Kenzie?" she asked. "What do you think about this idea?"

"Florida is nice," Kenzie said, grinning from ear to ear. "They've got Disney World."

A round of chuckles went through the adults. "Yes, they do," Sam said. "And the area I'm thinking we could move to is only about an hour away." He picked up a tablet computer and tapped on its screen for a moment. It lit up with a view of a house on a beach, and he turned it around so the rest of them could see it.

"Five bedrooms, six bathrooms, and over two hundred feet of our own private beach," he said. "I found this place for sale, and the price isn't nearly as bad as some of the others you'd find in the area on the beach. The place is freshly remodeled and ready to move in." He turned the tablet so they could all get a good look at it, sliding through several photos. "It's a small town, called Flagler Beach, only about five thousand people and a small school for the kids, but there's all the shopping we could ever need within a twenty-minute drive." He leaned close to his wife. "With everything we've saved over the past few years, we could pay cash for it, Indie, and still have plenty to reinvest and live on. What do you say?"

Kim cleared her throat, and Sam turned to look at her. His eyes narrowed as he waited for her to speak.

"Sam," she began slowly, "Beauregard says…"

"I didn't ask Beauregard's opinion," Sam said, glaring.

Kim grinned. "I don't think you're going to mind this one," she said. "He says your mother is jumping up and down with excitement."

Sam stared at her. While he was convinced that Grace really was hanging out with the old Civil War ghost, he was not entirely certain he believed everything Beauregard had to say about her. Still, his mother had always talked about moving to Florida someday. She probably was excited at the prospect.

"Okay, so that wasn't too bad," he said. He turned back to his wife. "Babe? What do you say?"

Indie looked at Sam, then at Kenzie and her mother, and a smile slowly spread across her face. "I think," she said, "that I hate the winters here even worse than you do. How soon can we go?"

Sam broke into a grin. "As soon as we get the house on the market." He turned to Kim. "And you'll need to decide what you want to do, of course."

Kim's expression went blank for a moment, and then she smiled. "I'm going to sell," she said. "If you guys leave, there's nothing else for me here, and Beauregard says Grace approves."

"Then it's settled," Sam said. "Let's get started today, shall we? And the first thing to do is to arrange to see that beach house!"

* * *

Sam had called that morning to arrange a viewing of the house a week later, and then they all got busy. One of the biggest realty companies in town had bought out Grace's brokerage, the money split between Sam and his sister, Carrie. Sam called them next and arranged for them to list both houses immediately, and the new owners were only too happy to oblige. Sam's house, which was in a nice neighborhood near some of the better schools, went on the market for a little over three hundred thousand, but Kim was shocked when they listed hers for almost three times that amount. Then it was time to start getting ready for the move. Kim chose a few things from the house that she felt (or was told) Grace would want her to keep, and then called an antique dealer to sell off the rest of the furnishings; Grace had been in love with antique furniture and was always buying new pieces. She had items that went all the way back to 17th-century New England, and Kim nearly fainted when the dealer offered her over forty thousand dollars for the lot.

Sam and Indie were a bit more conservative, especially since most of their furniture was nearly new. They packed boxes like crazy for the next three days, with Kim and Kenzie helping. When Indie commented that they were sure to forget what was in which box, Sam came up with the idea of using his phone to snap pictures as the boxes were packed, and then numbering them and taking another picture when it was closed up and sealed. He ended up with over three hundred pictures, but finding what they needed was not going to be that much trouble when the time came to unpack it all.

The moving company came a couple of days later, and everything was loaded into a semi-trailer, and then it was time to go. Rather than make the long drive, Sam had even arranged to have their cars transported, and he had called on Karen Parks, his closest friend from the police force, to drive them to the airport for the early morning flight. She showed up with a borrowed SUV that was big enough to carry everyone and their luggage, along with Samson, who was not a bit pleased about being trapped in his pet carrier.

"We're gonna miss you, Sam," Karen said as they made their way to Denver International. "You've been our go-to guy for a long time, now."

"You don't need me," Sam replied. "You're as good as I am, Karen, and you know it."

She looked at him in the rearview mirror as he sat in the back seat of her car beside Indie. "Yeah," she said, "sure I am. How many times did you have to save my ass?"

Sam chuckled.

They arrived a few minutes later, and Sam was just loading their bags onto a cart when he heard his name called.

"*Bloody hell, Prichard,*" came a familiar British accent, and Sam turned to find Denny Cortlandt hurrying toward him. He was followed by Summer Raines, Steve Beck, Walter Rawlings, Rob Feinstein, Ron Thomas and Jeff Donaldson.

"So, you thought you were going to slip away without a goodbye?" Summer asked. "You're a bad boy, Sam."

Sam grinned, accepted her hug and then shook hands with the men. "How did you guys find out?" he asked. "I was going to send you a postcard once we get settled in."

"Yeah, well, you should have told your wife," Steve said. "She announced it on your blog, and Walter spotted it last night. We couldn't let you get away without saying goodbye, Sam."

"So, this is really it?" Ron asked. "You really are retiring, and to *Florida*, of all places?"

"I am," Sam said. "And my hip says Florida is exactly where I need to be. Hey, don't be disappointed. You guys will always be welcome to come and visit, and we'll even have our own private beach."

Indie got a few hugs of her own, and Kenzie managed to sneak in several before they finally all said goodbye. Sam was touched to see that a few of them were misty at his departure, but he was really surprised when Rob Feinstein—one of the biggest, toughest men Sam had ever known—hugged him at the last moment with tears streaming down his face. The big man did not say a word, but Sam worried for a moment that his ribs might never recover.

And then the family was alone as they made their way through security and up to the gate where their flight would soon depart. They had just enough time to grab lunch at one of the restaurants on the concourse, and then it was time for boarding to begin. With the time zone change, they landed in Jacksonville at just past eleven thirty, and Sam went directly to the Enterprise counter to pick up the SUV he had arranged before they had left. It turned out that the manager had recognized his name and knew exactly who Sam was, so the Nissan he was expecting was upgraded to a Cadillac Escalade.

"It's my pleasure, Mr. Prichard," the man said. "I've been following your blog for the last couple of years, but I never dreamed I'd ever get the chance to meet you. Could I possibly get your autograph?"

Sam blushed but obliged, and then they loaded the bags into the big car and headed south. Sam had arranged for them to occupy a three-bedroom beachfront vacation suite until they made the decision about the house, and the GPS told him that it was slightly over an hour's drive. Since it was rapidly approaching noon, they decided to stop for lunch along the way, but Kenzie was impatient to see the beach. As a result, they decided to stop at what Sam declared to be the nicest Chick-fil-A he had ever seen.

An hour later, they pulled in at the motel and checked in, then gave in to the demands of their daughter and everyone changed into swimwear. It was a short walk across hot sand to the beach, and the gently rolling waves were comfortably warm and refreshing.

As Kim and Kenzie played together in the water a little further out, Sam and Indie sat happily giggling at little Bo splashing away in the shallows. The big smile on his face told them that he heartily approved of his new environment.

Indie looked up at Sam. "I can't believe we really did this," she said. "On the other hand, I am sort of surprised we never thought of it before."

"I had to get past the feeling that I was needed," Sam said. He looked off toward the horizon for a moment, then turned back to his wife. "When you keep getting told what a hero you are, it starts to go to your head, no matter how sensible you try to be. My ego was enjoying it all." He shook his head. "It wasn't until I realized how much it was all costing us that I knew it was time to throw in the towel."

"It almost cost us you, Sam," Indie said. "We weren't sure you were going to make it last time, and I just don't think I could have gone on without you." Sam saw the single tear that formed in the corner of her left eye.

"You would have," he said. "The kids would've needed you, so you would've survived. Eventually, you would've found someone else and gone on with your life, but I understand what you're saying. I couldn't imagine life without you, either."

She leaned against him. "But that is all behind us, now," she said. "Now it's just time for us."

The following morning, they kept their appointment to view the house. A real estate agent was waiting for them when they arrived.

"Mr. Prichard?" she asked. "I am Regina Bowman, we spoke on the phone last week."

Sam reached out and shook her hand. "Sam Prichard," he said, "and this is my wife, Indie, her mother Kim, our daughter Mackenzie and our son, Bo. It's a pleasure to meet you."

"Oh, no, the pleasure's all mine," Regina said. "I will confess I didn't recognize your name when you gave it to me, but one of the other agents in our office did. We did a little research to determine that you really are the Sam Prichard from the 'Adventures of Sam Prichard' blog, and then he made me read up on you. I have to say it is an honor to meet you, and I am delighted to meet your family." She handed Sam a card, then motioned toward the front door of the house. "Shall we?"

Sam knew it was a sale the moment they stepped inside. They entered the great room that went all the way through the house, culminating in a view of the ocean through a hurricane wall, a series of sliding glass doors that was almost twenty feet wide. When all of them were opened, the back of the house was open to the deck, which was screened in.

As Sam had seen online, there were five bedrooms, each with a bathroom of its own, and an additional large bathroom on the first floor. The master bedroom—Sam thought it should be called a suite, rather than a bedroom—was on the first floor and comprised a total of four rooms, counting its incredible bathroom. One of the rooms would be ideal for an office, Sam thought, but he was sure his wife would have other ideas for them.

Kenzie surprised them by insisting she wanted the smallest of the upstairs bedrooms, mostly because it was toward the front of the house and had a pair of dormers with small window seats under them. She thought they would be a wonderful place to sit and do her writing, something she had picked up from her mother in recent months.

Another bedroom was chosen for Bo, and Kim was allowed to take her pick. She took the one at the front of the house beside Kenzie's, but that didn't really surprise anyone. She and her granddaughter were very close.

The kitchen, according to Sam, looked like it belonged in a five-star restaurant. The range was gas and had three ovens and a total of ten burners on top, while the refrigerator was actually built into the wall and was divided into two sections. The first was much like a conventional refrigerator, but the other side was a walk-in cooler. There was a large freezer section in there as well, causing Sam to joke about going deer hunting.

There were two large living rooms, and it seemed almost every room except the bathrooms and kitchen had a fireplace. Regina assured them that they were fully working fireplaces, though they were set up for gas logs at the moment. All it took to burn wood, however, was to simply turn off the gas valves underneath each of them.

By the time they got to the point of discussing the purchase, it was getting close to lunchtime. Sam suggested they visit a local restaurant and eat while they talked business, and Regina suggested a place that was only half a mile away.

Having lunch took an hour. Agreeing on a price, with Regina calling the seller to get their feedback, only took fifteen minutes. Sam wrote a check for earnest money and agreed to have the balance of the purchase price bank wired the following day.

Two days later, they were given the keys and all of the paperwork. The house on the beach was theirs, and Sam called the movers. All of their belongings were already sitting just down the road in Daytona Beach, the truck having arrived the day before. It would all be delivered the following morning, and they could finally get settled into their new lives.

That had been nearly four months earlier, and they had been some of the happiest months of Sam's life.

Or at least they would have been, if it wasn't for that empty spot deep down inside of him.

TWO

Detective Garza was exhausted. After the events of the night before, he had found himself staying at the hospital until well past daybreak, shocked when three more victims of the same strange affliction were brought in. The doctors had been stymied as they tried to figure out what was causing the symptoms they were seeing, which included bleeding from every orifice and death within only minutes after the first manifestation.

"Doc," Garza had said that morning, "you gotta give me something. Just tell me this is some kind of disease and then I'm out of your hair."

Doctor Regalia, a swarthy Hispanic man himself, looked at him through bleary eyes. "Ed, I can't tell you that," he said. "At this point, we don't have any idea what's causing this. The primary symptom seems to be a breakdown of the endothelium, the lining of the blood vessels. That causes the blood vessels to become leaky, so the blood actually passes right through them. It can get into other parts of the body, including the area behind the eyes, nasal passages, and behind the eardrum, and the pressure builds up significantly until it forces its way out. It gets into the bladder, the guts, and that is how it comes out through the rectum and the urethra." He sighed and ran a hand over his face. "It could be some sort of virus or bacterial infection, but we can't find anything in any of the victims to give us that indication. Unfortunately, we also can't find anything that could be an external cause, so I don't know what to say."

"External cause?" Garza asked. "What kind of external cause are you talking about?"

"Well, any kind of poison or chemical exposure, maybe a radiation exposure. A large dose of anticlotting medication could conceivably cause this reaction, but none of these people seem to have any of those substances in their systems. I don't know what would cause the kind of bleeding these folks are exhibiting, but it doesn't really matter since we haven't found anything we can point to." He leaned against the wall and shook his head. "I don't know, Ed; this has got us all stumped."

Garza stared at him in silence for several seconds. "Poison? Do you really think it's possible somebody did this to these people deliberately?"

"Until I know what has caused these symptoms, and we have some idea as to how it was vectored—how they came in contact with it, that is—I have to say it's possible, but I haven't seen anything to indicate that is the actual reality. I honestly just don't know, Ed. Hell, for all I know, we could be looking at some sort of biological terror attack."

Garza's eyes were wide and his face went instantly pale. "Is that what you think it is?"

Regalia spread his hands. "I don't think it's anything," he said. "I can't form an opinion of any kind, I simply don't know enough. We've got CDC people flying down from Atlanta, and all I am hoping for the moment is one of them has run across something like this, somewhere in the world. At least then, we might have some idea of what it is, even if we don't know how to treat it." He laid a hand on the detective's shoulder. "Ed, go home and get some rest. I promise that as soon as we know something, we'll let you know.

Now, go, on doctor's orders. And give my love to Carmen."

Garza shook his head and ran a hand over his face. "Yeah, home," he said. "I have to get back to my office. If I don't get a report in on this this morning, the chief will have my head."

He had walked out of the hospital and gone to his car, but he just sat behind the wheel for several minutes before he started the engine. In his mind, he was trying to formulate just what he would put into his report, but none of it was making any sense. People who seemed perfectly healthy would suddenly start feeling disoriented, and a moment later, they would begin bleeding from their eyes. Bleeding from the nose and mouth came next, but then blood seemed to be coming from every bodily orifice. Even scabs would suddenly break open and begin to bleed for no apparent reason. Whatever it was, it was almost like it was blowing out even the smallest blood vessels, letting blood run freely like water.

"Shit," Garza muttered, and then he reached up and started the car. There was no other option but to head for the office and make his report. At least the drive would take a few minutes, allowing him to think about how to put all of this into words.

His cell phone rang and he wearily pulled it from its holster on his belt. "Garza," he said.

"What the hell is going on out there?" came a familiar voice. Captain Harrison was the chief of detectives. "Ed, we've got two more cases already this morning. Are you coming up with any ideas on what's happening?"

"Nada," Garza said. "The doctors don't have a clue, and they've even reached out to the CDC for help. Right now, they seem to think it's some kind of disease, but they aren't ruling out bioterror. It's even possible we are dealing with some kind of poison, but nobody has any idea what kind of poison could cause what we are seeing."

Harrison echoed Garza's earlier curse. "CDC? Hell, we are

probably going to end up in some kind of quarantine. How soon will you be back here? We need to talk to the chief, and I'm not doing it alone."

Garza let out a sigh. "I'm on the way," he said. "Probably another ten minutes or so. Want me to write my report first or just come straight to your office?"

"I think this is one report the chief is going to want straight from the horse's mouth," Harrison said. "Unfortunately, that makes you the horse."

"Yeah, yeah. Okay, I'll be there as soon as I can." Garza cut off the call without waiting for a goodbye, then punched the steering wheel. So far, they had eleven patients in the hospital with the same symptoms, and now two more cases had turned up? Whatever it was, it was going to be bad, and Detective Ed Garza felt certain that it was far beyond his investigative abilities.

Lately, he had come up with a mantra that helped him when he got stumped, and he felt it was time to resort to it once again. He eased his foot onto the brakes as he came up to a stoplight, then briefly closed his eyes and muttered, "What would Sam Prichard do?"

Garza had been attached to the Florida Anti-Terrorism Taskforce back when he'd first heard of Sam Prichard. That was when Sam had stopped a terrorist from tossing a small nuclear bomb into Lake Mead, an event that would have basically destroyed much of the Southwest. Despite attempts by the government to keep it quiet, CNN had gotten hold of the story and Sam had become a household name.

Shortly after that, Sam's wife had begun publishing a blog about his adventures, and someone had sent Garza an email with a link to it. He had become a regular reader, and considered himself to be one of Sam's biggest fans. When a homicide a couple of years earlier had left him without any viable leads, he had first asked himself that rhetorical question, and then he had sat down and tried to think through the case the way Sam might.

It had worked. One of the things that occurred to him was that the killer had to have known details about the victim's home that were rather obscure, and that led him to check out what kind of repairs had been done to the place in the past few months. To do so, he had spoken to the victim's friends and neighbors, and learned that the victim had once mentioned to a neighbor that a handyman had made some unwelcome advances toward her. She had fired the guy and apparently never mentioned it again, so it hadn't come up in their initial interviews.

A careful look at that handyman showed Garza that he had been called a stalker by a few other prior clients, so he checked the guy's cell phone GPS records and found that he had been in the vicinity of the victim's home the night of the murder. It was the first time this particular man had ever been questioned about the killing, and his nervousness told Garza that he was on the right track. After more than three hours of hammering at the guy, he finally broke down and confessed.

Since then, whenever a case seemed to be slipping away from him, Garza had resorted to the same mantra. For the rest of the drive back to the station, he tried to look at this new situation through Sam Prichard's eyes.

Unfortunately, it did not seem to be helping this time.

* * *

Garza and Harrison stepped into the office of the chief of police and were ushered directly inside by the receptionist. Chief Robert Olson was on the phone as they stepped inside, but he quickly ended the call and turned to look at them.

"Okay, give me what you got," he said.

Harrison looked at Garza meaningfully, and the detective cleared his throat.

"So far, we've got a total of at least eighteen victims," he said. "All of them are in critical condition at local hospitals, and all of them are showing similar symptoms. They seem to be perfectly healthy one moment, then suddenly they get disoriented and start bleeding from the eyes. Within minutes, they seem to be bleeding from every possible orifice and collapse. The doctors don't have any idea what's causing it, but the blood loss is so rapid that the only treatment they have come up with so far is to keep shoving more blood back in. As far as I know, they haven't identified any kind of infection that could be causing it, they don't know of any kind of poison or chemical that could do this sort of thing, and that leaves us with basically nothing to go on. The CDC is sending people in today, but one doctor did tell me that we could be looking at some sort of bioterrorism attack. He stopped short of saying that's what it is, but nothing else presents itself as an alternative."

Olson rubbed a hand over his bald head. "Dear God," he said. "If the CDC gets involved, this could turn into a major disaster. The last thing we need is for word to get out that we have an uncontrollable disease running through the city, but it's already starting to hit the news stations." He looked the two men in the eye. "We have no comment to make to the press, do you guys understand that?"

"Yes, sir," both of them said.

"Now, is there anything else you can tell me? The mayor is going to be on me any minute now—I want to be able to tell her something."

"I don't know what it would be, sir," Garza said. "I doubt this is anything that anybody has seen before, so we are in uncharted territory."

Harrison stayed silent, even when the chief looked directly at him.

After a moment, Olson shook his head and turned back to Garza. "Well, don't just stand here," he said. "Get busy and find me some answers."

"Sir," Garza said, "I can write my report, but then I need to get some sleep. I was up all night, and..."

"And we might be up for a few more nights before this is over," Olson said. "I'm sorry, Ed, but I need all hands on deck for this one."

Garza thought about protesting, but knew it would do no good. "Yes, sir," he said. He turned and walked out of the office, leaving Harrison standing there to take whatever ire the chief might have left.

He sat down at his desk and turned on the monitor for his computer terminal, then began typing up his report. When he was finished, he had a page and a half of basically nothing, but he printed it out dutifully and put it into the file folder he had begun on the case. His only real hope was that they would find out it was some sort of natural disease, something that could be cured. Unless that happened, Ed Garza and every other man and woman on the police force were going to lose an awful lot of sleep.

He took his phone out of its holster again and called his wife, Carmen. She was a good wife for a cop, he always said, because she never bothered him unless there was a genuine emergency of some sort.

"Hey, Ed," she said. "I noticed you didn't come home all night. Are you okay?"

"I'm fine," he said. "A little tired, though. We've got something weird going on, some sort of illness attacking people quickly and without warning. We don't know what it is, so I want you to be careful and stay home today. Try not to be around a lot of people, okay? Just in case this thing is contagious, somehow."

She was quiet for a couple of seconds. "And you've been around it?"

"I was at the hospital, where they were taking people. Hector Regalia says it doesn't look like it's too contagious at the moment, so he thinks I'm okay. If it was easy to catch, half the hospital would probably be sick by now. I don't think there's really much to worry about, but I would just rather you stay home as a precaution. Okay?"

"Okay," she said. "I had a hair appointment, but I can reschedule that. What about the kids, should I keep them at home today?"

"I'd rather you did. Just tell them I said so, they won't argue."

Like many couples, they ended the call with words of their affection for each other, and then Garza put the phone down on his desk. He turned again to the computer and logged in to his browser to pull up the Sam Prichard blog. Perhaps reading his hero's latest adventure might give him some new insights.

Unfortunately, he hadn't had time to check the blog the last few months. He had been extremely busy, and had simply not taken the time to pay attention to what was going on in Sam's life. The title of the latest blog post, therefore, caught him completely off guard.

> *A Fond Farewell*
> *by Indiana Prichard*
> *Well, the time has finally come. Sam is officially retiring, and we are settling in to our new lives. It has been a great run, and we have enjoyed sharing all of his adventures with everyone, but it is time for us to dedicate ourselves to our family. We wish everyone the best, and I might even continue to update this blog from time to time with hopefully less exciting tales of the wonderful things life holds in store for us.*
> *God bless everyone,*
> *Indie*

Garza sat there and stared at the screen for several moments, absolutely shocked and possibly a little heartbroken at the thought of his hero hanging up his shoulder holster. He was just about to close out the browser when he noticed the little flashing icon in the upper right that said, "UPDATE." He clicked it and another page opened up.

Exciting News

I guess it just goes to show that you never know what's coming next. A little over a week ago, Sam looked at me and suggested we move away from Denver, to a beautiful beach house he had located in Florida. He showed me the pictures and—well, I fell in love with it instantly. We are all packed up and ready to go, and we are actually getting on a plane early tomorrow morning to head for those sunny shores. If all goes well, we will be moving in by the end of the week.

Another entry followed that one, dated a week later.

All Settled In

Hey, everyone! Sure enough, we bought the house on the beach and we are pretty much moved in. I am sure we'll be unpacking boxes for the next month or so, but Sam came up with an interesting system so that we know which box has what, so it's not as bad as it sounds. We've been spending a little bit of each of the last few days splashing in the water on our own private stretch of beach, and Kenzie and Bo both love it. Sam says the warm saltwater is definitely helping his hip, and he hasn't even used his cane the last couple of days. That alone is worth making this move, but just enjoying our time together is the best benefit.

And then there was another paragraph, dated a month after that one.

The Joys of Retirement

I hope you read the above with a hint of skepticism. Anyone who has retired from something they enjoy doing probably has already figured out just how bored poor Sam has become. Don't get me wrong, he does his best not to let me see it, but I've known him for a while now. He is itching to do something exciting, so I am racking my brain trying to think of something that might fill that need for him. Anybody got any suggestions?

There were several more such entries over the past few months, but there was one at the bottom of the page dated only two days earlier. Garza scrolled down to it quickly, an idea forming in his mind as he did so.

Boredom Sucks

Sam has been really wonderful about everything, but it has finally dawned on me that he just isn't ready for actual retirement. No matter how he tries to simply enjoy life, there is something missing for him now, and it's become painfully obvious to me. As much as I hate to admit it, I've come to the conclusion that he's going to have to go back to doing something in the line of investigative work, but I haven't had the courage to discuss it with him yet. Hopefully, all of you will keep me in your prayers as I try to think of something he could do that won't put him into the terrible dangers he has faced before.

The grin that broke out on Garza's face might have frightened some people. He closed the browser and immediately started searching the state driver's license database. It took him only moments to find Sam's new Florida driver's license, along with his address.

It isn't often that a man gets to meet his hero. Garza checked on Google maps and found out that Sam lived less than an hour and ten minutes away. He hurried into Harrison's office and explained that something had come up, and he needed to take the rest of the day to follow a potential new lead.

Harrison did not even ask what it was.

THREE

Indie stepped out onto the deck a short time later, with a cup of coffee of her own, and sat down beside Sam.

"What are you thinking?" she asked, following his gaze out over the water.

"How much I love it here," Sam replied. He turned and smiled at her. "And how much I love you."

She grinned at him. "Yeah, sure," she said. "I bet you say that to all the girls."

"All the ones that matter," Sam said. "Oh, wait, that is only you." He leaned over to get a kiss and she obliged.

"Sam," Indie said hesitantly, "there is something I've been wanting to talk to you about. Is—is now a good time?"

Sam raised an eyebrow. "I'd say it's probably as good a time as any," he said. "What's on your mind, babe?"

"You. Sam, you've done everything you can to keep me from seeing it, but I can tell you are going nuts just sitting around here. You miss the work, don't you? Being a private eye, I mean."

Sam started to protest, but the look in her eyes told him it was time to be honest. "Yeah, sometimes," he said grudgingly. "I don't miss getting shot, of course, and I don't miss being away from my family so much, but—I guess I miss the chance to make a difference, does that make any sense?"

Indie smiled. "It does," she said. "And I've been thinking about what you could do about it. Have you thought about maybe talking to the police department here? I know it's small, but with your record, I'm sure they'd find a spot for you."

"Yeah, they probably would," Sam said. "But I don't think that would really give me what I'm craving. I even thought about maybe applying to the sheriff's office, maybe try to be a detective again. Even with the bad hip, I'm not completely crippled. Considering the last few years, I don't think it would keep me from working for them."

Indie sucked on her bottom lip for a couple of seconds, then smiled again. "If that is what you want to do," she said. "I love you, Sam, and I support whatever you decide. Just remember that it's a good size county, and you might be running all over it."

"I haven't decided to try it," he said. "It's really just been a thought. I don't know where else I might fit in, but I'm still thinking over possible options." He looked closely at her. "You're not upset with me, are you? For not talking to you about it, I mean?"

She shook her head. "No, Sam. I figured you would bring it up when you were ready, but it was so obvious that I decided to jump into the fire myself. Mom has noticed it, too, and I am pretty sure Kenzie has. She might not understand what it is, but she can tell that something is bothering you."

Sam nodded, then turned to look out over the ocean again. Maybe it was time to look into some possibilities. As long as he was not dealing with terrorists and international criminals, it would probably be fun.

* * *

It was still summertime, so Kenzie was out of school. She was enjoying the opportunity to sleep in a little later, and finally came down the stairs a little after ten o'clock that morning. She was followed a moment later by her grandmother, Kim, who was also sleeping a lot lately. The two of them had a tendency to spend a few hours a day in the water, and that left them tired enough to sleep well every night.

They walked into the kitchen to find Sam and Indie sitting at the table. Bo was in his high chair, sippy cup firmly clamped into his mouth while Indie was trying to feed him applesauce. Sam had his own laptop open and was reading something online, but he closed it quickly when they stepped into the room. Kim looked at him suspiciously, but Kenzie simply climbed up into a chair and looked at her mother.

"What's for breakfast?" she asked.

"Well, we were waiting for you guys," Indie replied, "because we were thinking about going out for breakfast. Anybody interested?"

Kenzie flared into a brilliant smile. "I am!" she said. "Can we go get waffles?"

"Hey!" Sam said quickly. "Nobody makes waffles like Mommy. We could go somewhere we can get eggs and sausage, wouldn't that be fun?"

Kenzie nodded. "Sure, as long as they have waffles."

"Give it up, Sam," Kim said. "She's been talking about waffles since she got out of bed this morning."

"Okay, fine, we can go to the Waffle House. At least there I can get steak and eggs. You guys can eat waffles if you want to, but I still say nobody makes them like Indie."

They all started getting ready to go, with Indie taking Bo to get him cleaned up and properly dressed. Sam only had to change shirts and slip on some shoes, and Kenzie and Kim had gotten dressed before they even came downstairs. It only took a few minutes for them to get ready, and then they headed toward the door.

Sam had almost reached it when the doorbell rang, and they all froze and looked at one another. They hadn't met that many people since arriving in town, and nobody was expecting visitors. Indie shrugged, so Sam opened the door to find a nice-looking Hispanic man standing there.

The man's eyes opened wide and he stared at Sam for a moment before breaking into a large grin.

"Hello," Sam said. "Can I help you?"

"Man, I sure hope so," the fellow said. "Mr. Prichard, my name is Ed Garza, and I am a detective with Orlando PD. I was hoping you might have a little time that we could talk."

Sam blinked, then glanced at his wife. Indie grinned and nodded, so he turned back to Garza.

"As long as you let me buy you breakfast," he said. "We were just heading out to grab a bite to eat."

Garza did a double take, then quickly nodded his head. "Yeah, sure, I can follow you, if that's okay. But why don't you let me buy you breakfast, instead? I'll be happy to pick up the tab."

Sam grinned and stepped out the door, holding out a hand to shake with Garza. "No, this is my pleasure," Sam said. "My friend, you may be the answer to a prayer."

* * *

From the house, the restaurant was only about ten minutes away. It was on A1A, the highway that ran along the coast, and Sam had declared it one of his favorite breakfast spots shortly after they moved in. At that particular time of morning, it was almost empty, so they were able to shove a couple of tables together and make one that was big enough for all of them.

Sam insisted they wait until their orders were in, then turned to Garza as the waitress walked away.

"So," he said. "How long have you been a detective?"

"Well, sir," Garza began, but Sam cut him off.

"Don't even start with that 'sir' crap," he said. "The name is Sam."

Garza grinned sheepishly. "I've been at this for almost six years, now. Took me a few years to make detective, mostly because I kept having little setbacks when I was in uniform."

Sam leaned back as the waitress set coffee in front of him, then he picked it up and looked at Garza again.

"Setbacks?"

"Yeah," the detective said with a grin. "Once, I arrested our congressman, got him for speeding. Another time, when I caught the mayor climbing out of a car that had just T-boned another one and realized he was drunk, I handcuffed him and made him wait until I checked on the people in the other car. The way I heard it, it's never a good idea to arrest the politicians. Both of those times, I was up to take the test for detective, and both times I got set back a couple of years, so I guess there's some truth to that."

Sam chuckled. "Yeah, there usually is. So, you said you hope I can help you. What's the problem?"

Garza looked around the table and suddenly wanted to be cautious about just how much he said. The thought of ruining breakfast for the ladies, including Kenzie, made him wonder if Sam might toss him out on his ear.

Despite his determination to act professional, Garza broke into a goofy grin. "Okay, Sam," he said. "Well, we have a case that is brand new, but it's already got us all—well, scared. We just don't know what it is, or how to even start to try to figure it out." He glanced at Indie and her mother again, then turned back to Sam. "I'm afraid the details are somewhat—disturbing, I guess would be the word. I don't want to go into them while these lovely ladies are trying to eat."

"Go for it," Indie said. "None of us are squeamish, I promise you."

Sam nodded. "She's right," he said. "I don't think there's anything you can say that is going to upset them."

Garza swallowed hard, then shrugged. "Okay, then," he said. "It started last night. The first victim was a young woman at a nightclub, dancing and just having fun. All of a sudden, and I mean with no warning at all, she became disoriented and stumbled, then began bleeding from her eyes. A moment later, blood was coming from every possible orifice, if you understand what I am saying."

"Even out of her butt?" Kenzie asked, looking calmly at Garza.

The man blushed, but nodded. "I'm afraid so, miss," he said. He swallowed again, then turned back to Sam. "She was rushed to the hospital, where she is currently in critical condition. Unfortunately, since then, we have had a total of eighteen or more people suffering from the same affliction. The doctors have no idea what it is. They can't find any kind of disease that could have these symptoms, so they have been looking at poisons. Still no idea what it could be, but whatever it is, it's very serious and very deadly."

Sam shoved a forkful of eggs into his mouth and looked closely at Garza. "Do you think it's poison?"

The detective rolled his eyes. "Sam, I will be honest and tell you that I don't know what to think," he said. "This thing has got me stumped."

Sam took another bite, then looked up again. "Detective Garza…"

"Oh, no," Garza said. "It's just Ed."

Sam grinned. "Okay, Ed," he said. "I guess the first question I want to ask is why the police are so deeply involved. This sounds more like the kind of thing that should be some sort of government investigation."

"Well, the CDC is supposed to be taking over, I guess," Garza said. "My problem is that I was there last night, I saw what these people were going through. I'm not the least bit ashamed to say that it scared the…" He looked sideways at Kenzie, then at her mother, then turned back to Sam. "Scared the willies out of me. Now, I ain't no doctor and I sure don't know nothing about no poison, but my gut—my gut tells me that somebody is behind this. Somebody, somewhere, is doing whatever is causing this, and that scares me even more than what I saw at the hospital."

Sam's eyes were locked onto his, the fork frozen halfway to his mouth, but as Garza finished speaking, he lowered the fork back down to the plate.

"I know about the gut," he said. "And I will trust the gut of a police detective over just about anything. You've been doing this job long enough to know when your gut is telling you straight. Tell me the whole thing, start from the beginning."

Garza did, telling Sam about the first call that took him to the hospital to observe Krista Harmon, the first victim they were aware of, and then continuing to talk about the rest of the night and the other victims who had come in. He recounted his numerous conversations with the doctors and nurses, and the hope everyone was expressing that it would turn out to be some new illness that was treatable.

"What about fatalities?" Sam asked. "How many have died from this thing, whatever it is?"

"As of the last I heard, no one had died," Garza said, but then he shook his head. "I've been out of touch for a few hours, though. That may have changed."

Sam nodded slowly. "I understand," he said. "Can you check? If anyone has already died from this, we need to know it."

Garza nodded and took out his phone, but looked at Sam. "I will find out," he said, "but how does that make any difference?"

"It's been less than twenty-four hours since it began," Sam said.

"If it can be fatal in that short a time, then we have a much bigger problem. That would make it one of the deadliest potential attacks we've ever known."

Garza's thumb ran over the keypad quickly, but his eyes never left Sam's face. "Then you agree with me? It sounds like some kind of poison, something somebody is doing deliberately?"

"I don't know enough to agree or disagree," Sam said. "But like I said, I trust the gut of a policeman."

Garza put the phone to his ear. "Denise? It's Ed. What's the situation with people at the hospital?" He listened for a moment, and then his face suddenly seemed to collapse in on itself. "Okay," he said. "Thanks. No, just tell him I'll be in tomorrow morning. I still haven't made it home to get any rest, yet."

He ended the call and put the phone down on the table. "There are now a total of thirty-six victims who show the same symptoms. Out of those, five have died. One of them was the first girl, Krista Harmon. She died about an hour ago, but she was not the first. That was an elderly man."

Sam looked at him, and a chill went down his spine. Without knowing exactly why he did it, he turned to his mother-in-law and saw the blank expression she wore when Beauregard was forcing his way forward.

"Samuel," she said, her voice sounding Southern and somehow deep. "You are going to need to be careful with this one. You need to remember that nothing is as it seems, and everything you believe to be true may turn out to be wrong."

His eyes wide, Sam looked at her for another moment. "Can you give me any hints?" he asked.

Kim blinked, then her face softened again. She saw Sam looking at her and gave him a sheepish grin.

"Sorry, Sam," she said. "He is gone."

Sam turned back to Garza and saw the confused expression on his face. "Don't ask," he said. "Just, please, don't ask."

Garza nodded, his eyes big and round. "No problemo," he said. "Was that Beauregard?"

Sam turned his face and looked at Indie, who shrugged and stuck out her tongue at him. "You honestly wrote about Beauregard on the blog?" he asked.

"Of course," she said. "How many times did he save your life, or give you a clue that took you in the right direction? You have to give credit where credit is due, Sam."

"I told her it was okay, Sam," Kim said. "I'm not ashamed of Beauregard, you know. He has helped me through some of the worst times in my life."

Sam rolled his eyes as he turned back to Garza. "That was Beauregard," he said. "And if you know enough to know about Beauregard, then you probably know that he's never been wrong. If he says nothing is the way it seems to be, then that pretty well confirms there is a crime involved. Now it's up to us to help you find out who's behind it."

FOUR

In the ethereal realm where Beauregard existed—in other words, in the foggy, fuzzy recesses of the mind of one Kimberly Perkins—the old Civil War ghost turned his ectoplasmic head and looked at his roommate, or perhaps we should say head-mate. Over the last few years, up until Grace Prichard was killed, the old spook had watched her through the eyes of his hostess, often wishing that she had lived during the time when he was in the flesh. True, she could be annoying as hell, and she could fly off the handle into confused and usually hilarious bouts of hyperactivity caused by stress, but there was just something about her that he liked. Had they both been in the flesh, he would have considered the possibility that he was somewhat enamored of the lady. Being dead and existing only as a feature of his hostess's subconscious personality, he simply passed it off as a wistful fancy.

Then came that horrible evening when Sam's long-lost twin brother, Cameron, had showed up at his house and threatened them all. Poor Grace had been forced to shoot Cameron in order to save Sam, but Cameron had also fired his weapon and Grace had died. The shock of losing her had been more than Beauregard could bear, and he had surged forward to take over Kim's body and kneel over her as she lay bleeding. He had heard her final words to Sam, and

41

despite the fact that he had no heart, it began to break.

His eyes, however, could see what no one else could as Grace was freed from the bonds of her earthly home. Without even thinking about what he was doing, Beauregard had reached out to her, taking her own disembodied hand and causing her to see him for the first time in his own person.

When one dies, the energy that is the life force within them does not cease to exist. In this universe, energy can be neither created nor destroyed, but only changed from one state to another. While we live, that energy is the power source of the body; at death, it is released and becomes the disembodied soul of who we were.

To us, the new state of existence doesn't feel a lot different at first. We continue to think of ourselves, and therefore to appear to others who can see us, as having the same body we had just departed. There may actually be minor differences, because the new ethereal body is based on our perception of ourselves, rather than on the physical characteristics of the mortal coil. Blemishes are gone, signs of aging are reduced and we seem to be a somewhat better version of ourselves.

Grace suddenly saw Beauregard, and he looked like the antique photo they had once found of him, back when they were working on a case that involved some of his descendants. He was tall and handsome, with the typical Confederate soldier's mustache and goatee, and it took her only a couple of seconds to realize that she had transitioned from the mortal plane to the immortal.

"Beauregard?" she had asked. "Is that really you?"

"Indeed it is, my dear lady," Beauregard had said, and the deep timbre of his voice came through as she had never heard it before. "I fear that you have made done with all matters of the flesh, my dear."

Grace looked at him as the two of them stood just behind where Kim, Sam, Indie and little Kenzie knelt, weeping over what had been her earthly home for the last fifty-odd years. She looked down at her body and instinctively reached out to comfort her son, but her hand simply passed through his shoulder.

She stared at Sam for a second or two, then looked back at Beauregard. "They can't see me or hear me or anything, can they?"

"I'm afraid not," Beauregard said. "We exist on a different level, and it is only the bond I have had with Kimberly that has allowed me to make any communication with that plane at all."

Grace nodded and seemed to swallow. "What's going to happen to me now?" she asked. "I'm supposed to see a light or something, right?"

"There will be a light," Beauregard said. "I don't know when it shall come, but it will appear. At that time, you will have to make a choice. You can go to whatever awaits us away from this world, or you can choose, as I did, to remain. I tried to watch over my family and was able to do so for some time, but I was bound to the house in which I had died. It was not until Kimberly came to live there that I was released from that bond and became connected to her."

Grace looked down at her family again. "So, if I don't go, I will be stuck here forever?"

"I honestly don't know the answer. Perhaps you will, but if you choose to remain, I should like to try to bring you into my own bond with Kimberly." He actually looked a little embarrassed. "If that would please you, I should say. I will confess that it would be pleasant to have some company."

Grace turned to look at the body of her other son, Cameron. It took only a glance to know that he was dead, and she pointed to his body with her free hand. "What happened to Cameron? Where is he?"

Beauregard glanced at the body. "I'm afraid I don't know," he said. "I did not see him leave his body, and he apparently paid no attention to me. To be honest, all of my attention was focused on yourself."

She turned to look at him again. "Why, Beauregard," she said. "If I didn't know better, I would think you were blushing." She glanced down at where their hands were still clasped together. "If I could stay with you, at least I would still be close to my family. If we can do it, I am definitely willing. Besides, you're not all that bad-looking. If I had to spend a few years hanging around in Kim's head, I could at least enjoy the view."

A bright light suddenly appeared at the other end of the room, and both of them turned to look at it.

"It came quickly this time," Beauregard said. "Sometimes, it doesn't come for days or weeks. You must have achieved some measure of favor in Heaven."

Grace swallowed. "Is that what that is?" she asked him. "Is that the door to Heaven?"

"That is how I have always thought," Beauregard replied. "I confess that I have never seen what is on the other side, however." He turned to look at her. "I can tell you that this is not what everyone sees. For some, there is a great aperture of darkness, and those to whom it appears seem to have no choice about passing through it. I have seen numerous souls cry and weep as they seemed to be dragged by invisible bonds through that dark opening. I have never heard anyone express any kind of fear with this door, however."

"So, if I go through, I will probably find my late husband there?"

Beauregard lowered his eyes. "I would assume so," he said.

"And maybe my parents, and others of my loved ones who have already passed away?"

"I believe that may be the case, yes," Beauregard said, still keeping his eyes averted.

Grace stood silently for a moment, and then turned to Beauregard. She looked at their hands, still holding on to one another. "I can feel your hand," she said. "How can I feel your hand?"

"I have theorized that those of us who exist in this realm, being made entirely of energy, have as our form some sort of energy field. Our fields seem able to interact with one another, giving the sensation of touch."

Grace broke into a smile. "Good-looking, and smart, too?" She glanced back at the light. "If I don't go, will I ever get another chance?"

"It seems we do," Beauregard said. "I have seen souls step through when the light appears for others, and there is always a shout or a gasp as of great joy as they pass through."

Grace turned back to him. "Then I am not ready to go just yet," she said. "Maybe it's time to start teaching me about how to be a ghost."

The two of them stood by and watched the events of the rest of the evening, with the arrival of paramedics and police leading to the final statements about what had happened. They talked a little bit, but mostly they just stood quietly and watched as the people they both cared for dealt with their emotions.

Finally, it was time for everyone to leave. The house was being sealed as a crime scene, so the entire family was going with Kim back to what was now her own home.

"So, what do we do?" Grace asked. "Do we just automatically go wherever Kim goes?"

Beauregard looked at her, his face reflecting a bit of nervousness. "For me, it could be that simple. It takes an effort for me to be here, outside of her mind. You, on the other hand, have never been there. Hold tight to my hand, and let us find out what is going to happen."

Grace clung to him, but then she put a hand to his face and forced him to look at her. "Just one thing, Beauregard," she said. "If this doesn't work, you make sure they know that I am stuck in this house. You will do that for me, right?"

The old soldier smiled. "Immediately, my dear lady."

He turned away and took a step toward Kim, and the two of them faded away. A moment later, Grace opened her eyes to find herself in an entirely different world.

"Okay," Grace said. "Why does this look suspiciously like an old cabin?"

Beauregard blinked. "I suppose because I have created an environment in which I am most comfortable," he said. "It has honestly never occurred to me before that anyone else would ever be a guest in my humble abode."

Grace looked around the single room, furnished with what looked like hardwood chairs and a table with benches. There was a fireplace on one wall, but she did not see windows or doors.

"There is no way out?" she asked.

"I have never needed one," Beauregard said. "I learned long ago that I need only think of stepping outside, and I am there. To be frank, I have not done so often. Being out there amongst the living is lonely. At least, in here, I know that I can make Kimberly hear me."

Grace nodded. "But what happens when they leave the house? Will I still be with you in here, or will you simply vanish and I will be stuck in Sam's house all alone?"

Beauregard seemed to look off into space for a moment, and then he smiled as he turned back to her. "You will apparently remain with me," he said. "It seems that Ms. Kimberly is already in the back seat of Samuel's car, and we are somewhere on the highway. When I was trapped in my cabin, I could not so much as step out the door."

Grace sat down in one of the chairs, relief evident in her face. "Thank goodness," she said. "Loneliness is not something I've ever done well with. Why do you think I let Kim move in with me, even with what I was convinced was her insanity at the time?"

Beauregard smiled. "You are, of course, referring to the insanity of believing she had an old Confederate ghost living in her head?"

Grace gave him a mock glare. "Don't start with me," she said. "You may be dead, but I can still make your life miserable if I want to."

* * *

Life as a ghost was not like life as a living person. They did not sleep, did not eat and most of the time, they were only aware of the world around them as a sense of sounds heard softly in the distance. Beauregard showed Grace how to extend her consciousness outside the "cabin," so that she could see through Kim's eyes and even catch smells, tastes and sensations of touch. When Kim held Bo, for instance, Grace would smile and enjoy the feeling of her little grandson being so close.

In the quiet times, however, it became clear that they could touch and feel one another, and Grace came to accept his theory of "energy fields" that could interact with one another. They became playful, and the touches grew soft and lingering. It was probably inevitable that they would eventually think of being even more intimate with one another, and it was Grace who first suggested it.

"Wow," she said a little later. "That was nothing like I remember, but I'd have to say it was better! How did it feel to you?"

Beauregard looked at her. "Urp," he said. "Izza bah-boh…" He shook his head to clear it. "My dear, while I had never entertained the notion that such a thing was possible, I might say that I am very pleased we were together for the discovery."

The afterlife took on a new meaning for them after that, and they grew closer. Before long, they were sharing thoughts and barely needed to "speak" to each other; they were closer than any two living people could ever be, and it made them aware of each other in ways that no one else could possibly comprehend.

Grace found a place for herself in Beauregard's ethereal realm, and she sometimes marveled that she was not bored to tears. It seemed to her, and she said as much to Beauregard, that all of the parts of life that were unpleasant got left behind, while the wonder and joy and even the love she had known were still with her. Every minute seemed alive and exciting, even when they were only experiencing their strange reality as sitting quietly together.

Not everything was boring, though. Grace was able to help Beauregard with some of his predictions, and had been thrilled when they helped Sam solve a case and save the day. When Sam had almost been killed on his last active case, and was lying halfway between life and death, she had even been able to appear to him for a short time. Sam had only told Indie and Kenzie about the experience, and he insisted it was her annoying manner that pushed him to survive so he wouldn't be stuck there with her; nonetheless, it had finally settled all his doubts about Beauregard's reality.

She'd been delighted that Sam decided to retire, but it was not long before even she could tell he was restless. The move to Florida, where she had always told herself she was going to live someday, had helped for a while, but there was less spring in his step lately, less life in his face.

Like Indie, she knew that Sam needed to work. She had been thinking of trying to commandeer Kim herself to discuss it with her daughter-in-law, the way Beauregard sometimes did when he needed to make himself heard, but Indie had beaten her to it. Grace had been proud, but even she could never have guessed how soon the chance for Sam to return to work would come.

And now it was time, and the case being laid out before them all scared her to…

Well, it scared her.

FIVE

"Ed, tell me this," Sam said. "Do your superiors know that you came to see me?"

Garza gave a half grin and shrugged. "I didn't say anything to anybody—I wasn't even sure if you would see me. All I know is that somebody has to figure out what's going on here, and you're the only one I could think of who might be able to help."

"Then you don't have any official permission to bring me in on the case," Sam said. "That could be a problem."

"Look, Mr. Prich... Sam, I will pay you myself. I got some money in the bank and..."

"I don't want your money, Ed," Sam said. "I just want to help, but I can't get involved in a police investigation without permission from the department. What we're going to need to do is probably meet with your superiors first, then go up the chain of command to see if we can get that permission."

Garza left them shortly after they finished eating, and Sam promised to meet him the next morning at his office in Orlando. Sam and his family went home, and Indie joined him immediately in the little room he called his den, but she thought of as his office.

"Okay," she said. "First step?"

"Let's see what Herman can find related to the symptoms. We

know that whatever it is, it affects the lining of the blood vessels. What kind of things can do that?"

Indie set up the parameters for the search in her personal AI program, which she called Herman, and then turned him loose. The familiar chimes began going off almost instantly as he found relevant information, displaying links on the screen.

The first link went to a Wikipedia article about the endothelial cells and what could affect them. Possible causes included anticoagulants, inflammation and several other factors that could actually be related, but nothing indicated any sort of bleeding on the scale Garza had reported. Indie clicked another link, and they learned about chemicals that could damage the endothelial cells, but again, nothing indicated the massive amount of damage these victims seemed to be suffering.

An hour later, having looked at more than a hundred links that Herman had found, Sam sat back and shook his head.

"Whatever this is," he said, "it isn't something that medicine is commonly familiar with. We could be dealing with an entirely new kind of poison, and that makes me wonder if this could be some sort of bioterror event."

Indie looked at him. "Well," she said, "the CDC is already on this. Maybe they'll know more about it by the time you get there tomorrow."

"That's what I'm hoping," Sam replied. "If we can figure out what the cause is, then we can start looking for its source. I don't know any other way I can help on this but to go with the assumption that this is a planned, deliberate attack of some sort."

Indie looked at him for another couple of seconds, then turned and began tapping the keyboard once more. "I'm going to have Herman look for similar cases," she said. "If this is happening somewhere else, or if it's happened in the past, that may give us something to go on."

She hit the enter key to tell Herman to start searching, and then they sat back and waited for the chimes that indicated he had found something. When no chimes rang out for more than five minutes, Herman displayed a big question mark on the screen. That was his signal that he had found nothing to match the search parameters she had given him, and seeing it was a very rare event.

"So this is definitely new," Sam said. "And at the moment, it seems to be isolated to the Orlando area. That is the only good thing I see so far."

"But what if it is some kind of infection? A disease that can be transmitted from person to person? You're going to be heading right into the middle of it, Sam."

"My gut is telling me this is something chemical, something that somebody is introducing into the victims. It could be an injection, maybe something they eat or drink, but somehow, he's getting it into their bodies. If it was actually contagious, I think the people at the nightclub where the first girl came down with it would be showing some kind of symptoms."

"Not necessarily," Indie said. "Even if it is some kind of germ, we have no idea how long the incubation might take before symptoms appear. The people who suddenly started getting sick with it last night may have been infected weeks ago, Sam. Until they can figure out what the actual cause is, there's no way to know just how much danger you might be in down there."

"As surprising as it may be to hear me say this," Sam said, "I think Beauregard has already ruled that out. An infection would be the natural, logical thought with something like this, but he pointed out that nothing we believe to be true is likely to actually be so. I am going to trust that he still knows what he's talking about, even with Mom yakking away in his ear."

Indie reached out and took his hand. "I certainly hope so," she said. "So much for retirement, right?"

"I don't think I'm really coming out of retirement," he said, and then he grinned. "Or maybe I could. I could become a consulting detective, like Sherlock Holmes. Just let different agencies come to me when they're stumped."

She gave him a less than humorous grin and shook her head. "I just hope that'll be enough for you," she said. "I'd hate to think you're going to be disappearing on trips again all the time. And while I might be upset about it, I'm not sure Kenzie and Bo would ever forgive you."

Sam grinned back. "That's why I thought of being a consultant. If I'm just advising, I'm not as likely to end up in somebody's gun sights."

Indie shot him a dour look. "I guess I can see that," she said. "But please, Sam, just be careful. We do not need you out there risking your life all the time again."

"Don't worry, babe," Sam said. "I meant it when I said I was tired of getting shot."

Indie bit her bottom lip. "And I want to ask one more thing of you."

Sam cocked his head slightly and looked at her. "What's that?"

"It's Beauregard," she said. "Sam, I want you to talk to him more. Listen to what he has to say. I know he can be a pain in the butt, but he's always right. I'd just feel a lot better if you would include him in this."

Sam rolled his eyes slightly, but he smiled and nodded. "You got it," he said. "I'll talk to the spook."

* * *

Grace and Beauregard were sitting on air not far away, and she turned to look at him. "Did you hear that? Sam has agreed to pay more attention to you now."

Beauregard looked at her for a moment before he replied. "I have been thinking about this while they were talking. You know, my dear, since you came to be with me, we seem to be a bit less restricted than I was before. There may be more ways we can help him than my little hunches about the future."

Grace raised a ghostly eyebrow. "What do you have in mind?"

"My predictions come from some unknown source," he said. "However, as we can now move about more freely than I could in the past, I think it possible that we could help Sam to discover information he needs. Of course, we could only share the information directly with Kimberly, but she could then pass it on to him."

Grace turned toward him. "Do you really think that might work?"

Beauregard chewed the inside of his cheek for a second, and Grace wondered, as she often did, about his very lifelike mannerisms. "I would say it depends on a couple of things. In the past, I could not move more than a short distance away from Kimberly, but now you and I have been able to go into different rooms, even go outside of the house. I find that rather interesting. I wonder how far we can go."

Grace straightened herself out to stand on the floor. "Only one way to find out," she said. "Let's go for a stroll down the beach."

Beauregard smiled up at her as he got to his own feet, and then the two of them walked right through the back door. They crossed the deck and walked down the steps to the path that led down to the beach, and Grace held on to Beauregard's hand.

"I wonder why we can walk up and down stairs," she said. "I wonder why we don't just walk straight off into the air."

"I suppose that is because we remember walking," Beauregard replied. "These immaterial bodies of ours simply do what they have always done when they were encased in the flesh."

"I guess so," she said. "In the movies, it always looks like ghosts can fly. Have you ever tried?"

"Actually, we can. I simply do not think about it very often, but let us do so now."

He raised a foot as if he were going to step up onto something, and then it seemed like he pushed off from the ground. Grace felt herself rising along with him as she held his hand, and a moment later, they were floating a few feet above the path. They were still moving in the same direction, headed toward the beach.

"Well, you could've shown me that sooner," Grace said. "This is pretty freaky."

Beauregard smiled, having become accustomed to her outdated slang.

"I suppose it is, when you've not done it before. This is the farthest I have ever gone. Before Kimberly, I could not leave my old cabin, and once I was bound to her, I gave up trying. I have not done this in many, many years, but I suppose it is like riding a horse. Once you get the hang of it, you just never forget."

"Like riding a bicycle," Grace said. "That is how we say it nowadays."

Beauregard looked off to the south and they veered in that direction. Neither of them had any sense of how fast they were actually moving, but it seemed like they reached the next house, nearly a mile away, within just a minute or so.

"Well, we have come some distance," Beauregard said. "In the past, if I got too far from Miss Kimberly, I would feel as if I were being pulled back to her, strongly enough that I could not resist. It felt like a rope around my neck, almost like I was being hanged."

"Well, I don't feel anything like that," Grace said. "Do you?"

"No," Beauregard replied. "I will confess that this is an amazing feeling. Freedom, I suppose, is always something the human spirit yearns for."

"Well, freedom is all well and good, but then I start to wonder how long we can be out like this. Aren't we connected to Kim, somehow?"

"Indeed. Perhaps we should return."

They swung around in an arc, and were back at the house in what seemed only a matter of seconds. They settled onto the back deck and walked once more through the closed sliding doors.

Sam and Indie were still where they had left them, but they seemed to have lost interest in the computer. Sam was holding Bo, while Kim and Kenzie were sitting on the love seat Sam had picked up at a thrift store.

"Look at them, Beauregard," Grace said. "I don't think I have ever seen them so happy."

"I agree," he said, but then his face suddenly grew dark. "I only hope that it will last."

Grace turned to look at him. "What is that supposed to mean? Did you get another feeling?"

Beauregard nodded. "I did. I am afraid I've been made aware that our little family is not yet done with dangers. Samuel must find out who is doing this, and he must find out soon. This terrible illness is going to strike close to home, Grace. I cannot see who will be affected, but I know that Sam must solve the case to save them."

Grace's face was one of shock. "They're going to get this? This sickness, or whatever it is?"

"At least some of them," Beauregard replied. "More than one, but I do not know who. However, this makes it even more important for us to do all we can to assist Samuel. He must solve the case, Grace. It is the only way to save our family."

"Then shouldn't we tell them, now?"

Beauregard seemed to sigh. "As much as I despise the necessity, I suppose we must."

He took her hand once again and stepped toward Kim, and the

two of them vanished. A moment later, Kim's eyes went wide.

"Oh, Sam," she said. "Oh…"

Sam and Indie looked at her in surprise.

"Mom?" Indie asked. "What's the matter?"

Kim looked at her for a second, then turned to Kenzie. "Sweetheart? Would you take your little brother into the living room and find something on TV for you guys to watch?"

Kenzie looked at her parents. "I know what that means," she said. "That means she wants to talk to you about something she thinks I am too young to hear." She shot her grandmother a scornful look, then took her baby brother from Sam and left the room.

Sam looked at Kim. "Okay, what's that face about?"

"It's Beauregard," Kim said. "He just told me that some of us are going to be affected by whatever this is, and that the only way to save us is for Sam to crack the case as quickly as possible."

Indie turned to Sam, her face white and frightened. Sam was still looking at his mother-in-law.

"Does he know who? Or how soon? Anything he can tell me will help."

Kim shook her head. "He said he can't see those things, not yet, anyway. But he said—Sam, he says that he and Grace are going to be able to help. They can move around now in ways Beauregard never could before, so they can go places that maybe you can't."

Sam narrowed his eyes. "Go places? I thought they were stuck in your head?"

Kim shrugged. "Hey, I thought so too," she said. "Beauregard just told me it isn't that way anymore. They went down the beach a couple of miles just a little bit ago, he says, and didn't have any problem. They're going to stick close to you, at least as much as they can."

Sam stared at her for a few seconds, then turned to look at his wife. His face said everything that needed to be said.

SIX

Sam got up early the next morning and took the Mustang as he headed toward Orlando. The drive would last a little over an hour, and he wanted to make sure his head was clear before he got there.

Garza had called him the evening before to tell him that four more of the victims had passed away. Whatever the affliction was, it was definitely acting fast. Some of the people who had died had only been infected that morning. Hearing that news, Sam became doubly concerned about Beauregard's prediction.

He caught himself looking in the rearview mirror, trying to check the back seat to see if he had any ghostly passengers, but he knew it was futile. If they were tagging along, they still weren't going to be visible to him. The only time he had ever seen Beauregard and his mother was when he himself was lying at death's door. While he admitted to being convinced now that the old ghost was real, he just wasn't sure how they expected to be of any help in this case.

After all, Beauregard was from another century and time, and Grace was anything but an investigator. If they were tagging along, the best he could hope for would be that they could let Kim and Indie know if something happened to him.

The only new information Garza had been able to get him was that the CDC personnel had arrived, but even they were stumped. They had determined that the primary—and ultimately fatal—symptom was the breakdown of the endothelial cells in the blood vessels. It was not just concentrated to a single area like most such infections, however; all of the blood vessels were being affected about the same time.

Unfortunately, without knowing what was actually causing the condition, they could not even begin to guess how long it took to have such a deadly effect. The symptoms began almost simultaneously throughout the body, but there was no way to know how much time had passed since the cause was introduced to the victim.

Sam offered up a silent prayer that they might have learned something more overnight, something that could give him a lead, but he didn't actually hold out much hope for it. The problem was being examined by some of the brightest minds in the medical field, he was certain. If they weren't able to find an answer, he wasn't actually sure what he would be able to do.

He stopped at a convenience store and got some coffee and a doughnut, and spotted a newspaper. The headline was bold and dark: "CDC: Unknown Bleeding Sickness Strikes Local Citizens." Sam picked up a copy, then continued on his way. He pulled up at the Orlando police headquarters at a little after seven thirty, which was when Garza had suggested they meet up, so he climbed out of the car and used his cane lightly as he made his way into the building.

"Hi, can I help you?" The lady behind the desk smiled up as he entered.

"My name is Sam Prichard," he said. "I'm supposed to meet Detective Ed Garza this morning."

Her eyes became big and round. "Oh, yes, Mr. Prichard," she said. "Ed said you were coming, and I can't tell you what a pleasure it is to meet you. He's been talking about you for a couple of years, I think he got all of us reading your blog. He was so excited when he found out you were living in Florida, now."

Sam grinned. "That blog gets around," he said. "Is Ed here yet?"

"Sam," he heard, and turned to find Garza walking toward him. "Here I am."

Sam turned away from the broadly smiling receptionist and shook hands with the detective.

"And here I am," he said. "Any new developments yet?"

Garza shook his head. "Nothing I've heard about," he said. "Come on, they're waiting for us."

Sam nodded and followed as he led the way back into the bowels of the building. They passed through a door that required someone to buzz them in, and then down a long hallway. When they came to a door near the end of the hall, Garza opened it and motioned for Sam to precede him inside.

Two men wearing business suits were sitting at a round conference table, and both of them got to their feet as Sam entered, with Garza right behind him. The man who was closest held out a hand.

"Mr. Prichard? I'm Captain David Harrison, chief of detectives."

Sam took his hand and felt a firm grip. "Sam Prichard," he said. "A pleasure to meet you, though I wish it was under other circumstances."

The other man stepped forward and held out his own hand. "I'm Chief Robert Olson," he said. "Detective Garza told us that he had spoken with you, and that you were willing to try to help. Considering what we're up against, I can only express my gratitude."

"Again, Chief, it's my pleasure." He felt another firm grip as he shook hands with the chief of police.

"First things first, I guess," Olson said. "I have to submit your fees for approval. Do you have a set rate that you charge for situations like this?"

Sam blinked. "To be perfectly honest, I hadn't even thought

about it. Is there a standard rate?"

Olson glanced at Harrison, then back to Sam. "Well, there is, but I'm not sure it's worthy of a man of your abilities."

"I'm sure it will be fine," Sam said. "I'm comfortably retired, so this isn't about money for me. I'm just here to help, if I can, and if I can't, then I don't deserve to get paid, anyway."

Olson grinned. "Help like that I can take any time I can get it," he said. "Don't worry, I'll get it all submitted. Can we take a seat and talk a bit?"

"Of course," Sam said, taking his seat. The others all sat down and Chief Olson turned to Garza.

"Ed, you have the lead on this case," he said. "Why don't you start off?"

Garza cleared his throat. "Well, I think I got Sam pretty much up to speed on the case," he said. "We don't really know anything new, other than the fact that more people have died. There are forty-three cases in the hospitals right now, and a total of sixteen people have already passed away."

"Yes," Olson said. "I spoke with a Doctor Marissa Dione from the CDC this morning, and she says that this is unlike anything they've ever run across before. She did say she has hope they'll find the cause, but it's going to take some time."

"That is completely understandable," Sam said. "Since it's something entirely new, they can't just look in the back of the book somewhere. Can I ask what steps you have taken in the investigation so far?"

"I've been looking at the victims," Garza said. "Trying to find some common denominator, but so far I've come up with squat."

"There is nothing that ties them together?" Sam asked. "No place they all went to in the last few days?"

Garza shook his head. "Not that I can find," he said. "With this many people, there have been a few overlaps, but nothing that could affect all of them."

"What kind of overlaps?" Sam asked.

"Well, a few of them," Garza said, "and I am talking mostly about maybe a third of the ones we knew about yesterday, they all work in the same general area. Some of them work in a shopping center, and there's a couple of factories close by where two or three of the others worked. The rest of the people, though, they don't work anywhere near there, and they don't live around there, either. There just ain't anything I can find that connects them all together."

"Well, the fact that some of them work near each other is a place to start. We need to look at what else is in that area, some business or location that all of these people might have visited, even if only for a moment. Gas stations, convenience stores, there has to be someplace where all these people came into contact with whatever is causing this condition. Whether it's a disease, poisoning or maybe even some kind of radiation, in order for so many people to have the same condition, they all came in contact with the source at some point. If we can get some idea how that happened, we might find a way to determine how or where the whole thing started."

"I agree," said Harrison. "The chief and I have already assigned a number of uniforms to look for just such connections. Any idea what we should be doing in the meantime, while we're waiting for answers?"

"From what Ed has told me, I get the impression that none of the victims have been able to give you any information?"

Garza shook his head again. "None of them have been able to speak," he said, "and we have talked to their friends and family, but they don't have any idea where this might've come from."

Sam looked thoughtful for a moment. "Sometimes, the victims can tell us things even without being able to speak. If possible, I'd like to go out to the hospital and talk with the doctors and nurses. There may be something they observed that will help us track down the source, at least in some of the cases."

Olson glanced at Harrison and Garza, then turned back to Sam. "I think that might be an excellent idea," he said. "Detective Garza will go with you, if that's all right. Oh, and you might stop at the dispatch office. We have temporary police identification that we use for visiting police officers when they work with us. We should probably give you one, as well."

The four of them rose from the table and Sam followed Garza to the dispatch office, where he was handed a temporary police ID card. The card said that he was consulting with the Orlando PD and was to be accorded every respect and cooperation due to any other police officer. He signed for the card and tucked it into his pocket, then followed Garza out to the parking lot. The detective hit a button on his key fob and one of the dozen identical silver Dodge Chargers flashed its lights.

"That one's ours," Garza said, leading the way toward the car. They climbed in and buckled up, and Garza started the engine and put it into gear. They cruised slowly out of the parking lot and onto the street, turning right to head toward the nearest hospital.

"Orlando Regional is one of the biggest hospitals in the city," Garza said as he drove. "It's the one where most emergency cases get taken, especially if they happen really within the city. That's where I was at the other night, where most of the cases have been taken. There are a couple out at Advent, and one at Children's, but I don't even want to think about that."

"That was something I hadn't thought to ask," Sam said. "Only one child has been affected?"

"Yeah, so far," Garza said. "A little boy, he's only, like, twelve. I haven't seen him or talked to his family, I guess he just came down with it last night sometime. Everyone else is an adult, but some of them were pretty young, too."

"What about other demographics? Is there any preponderance of race, social status, financial status, anything like that?"

"We got a couple executives, and we got people who can barely make ends meet. We got people who live in fancy condos and another one who was homeless. We got whites, Cubans, black, everything. Nothing stands out."

"So age, race, employment and money don't seem to be factors. What else could we look at?"

Garza gave him a sour grin. "You know what I do when I get stumped like this?"

Sam looked at him and shook his head. "No, what?"

"I always ask myself what you would do," Garza replied. "You don't know it, but you have helped me solve a lot of cases the last couple years. The way you look at things different than the rest of us, you taught me a lot with your blog."

Sam shrugged, grinning. "You can thank my wife for that," he said. "She started that some time ago, and I didn't even know about it. I never really wanted to be famous; I was just a cop who wanted to do his job, until I got hurt bad enough they took me off the force and made me retire."

"And that's when you decided to become a private eye?"

"I don't know that I ever really decided to do that," Sam said. "I laid around and felt sorry for myself for a couple of years, but then one of my neighbors came to ask for my help because her granddaughter was missing. I had to have help with that one because a lot of what was involved was tied in to computers and stuff, and that's how I met my wife. She is pretty good with computers. I found the little girl, but I also blundered into a situation that was connected to national security. An old government agent and I had to make a stand, and we were lucky we even came out of it alive. After that, I guess it just felt good to be back in the saddle. Being a private eye meant a little extra income, but it also made me feel like I had a purpose again." He chuckled. "Okay, that's my story. What's yours?"

"Me? Family came here from Mexico a couple generations back. I grew up on the streets like a lot of Hispanic kids, but I lost some of my friends to drugs and overdoses. Decided I didn't want to be part of that world, so after a hitch in the army, I came back and applied to the police academy. Turned out I had a gift for getting the street kids to talk, so that helped me end up as a detective. Now I just try to keep my head above water. It's easy to drown in a city like this."

The hospital loomed ahead, and Garza put on the turn signal and followed the lanes into the parking lot. There was a section reserved for police and emergency vehicles, so he parked the car as close to the door as he could. The two of them climbed out and Sam used the cane lightly. The time he was spending in the ocean surf seemed to be helping his hip a lot lately, and he could go at least a couple of hours on his feet without experiencing terrible pain.

Doctor Regalia was standing in the middle of the ER lobby when they walked in, and he spotted Garza instantly. He turned away from the nurse he had been speaking with to approach the detective, his face set in a grim expression.

"Ed," he said. "Looks like I get to give you the news."

Garza froze and looked at his old friend. "What kind of news?"

"Some of the tests we have been running finally paid off," Regalia said. "We know what the cause of this is, now. That's the good news. The bad news is that there's no longer any doubt. This is some kind of biological attack. It seems to be localized here in Orlando, but the cause of this condition is chemically based. It is some kind of enzyme that actually dissolves the endothelial cells, and it works pretty quickly. Doctor Dione from the CDC says it probably takes less than three hours from the time the victim comes into contact with it for it to spread through the bloodstream, doing its damage all the way. By that time, there's enough breakdown for blood to be passing through the blood vessels, and then it's just a short time later that it starts forcing its way out."

"Holy mother of... What about treatment? Do they know what to do about it yet?"

Regalia shook his head. "Until they can identify exactly what chemicals are involved, there's not much hope of finding anything that is going to stop it. Come on, I'll take you to Doctor Dione and let her explain it to you."

Regalia glanced at Sam and Garza quickly made the introductions. The doctor shook Sam's hand and the three of them headed up the hallway.

SEVEN

"This is so frustrating," Grace said. "I don't know how we can help Sam when he doesn't even know we're here."

"I understand, my dear," Beauregard said. "However, we are at least in a position to learn things if the opportunity arises. We can get any information we find to Kimberly when we return home, so she can share it with Samuel."

Grace threw her hands in the air. "But there's nothing to learn," she said. "How are we supposed to learn anything about some mysterious disease that nobody understands?"

Beauregard watched Sam, Garza and the doctor as they spoke with a small woman in a white lab coat. "All we can do is pay attention for the moment. Let's hear what the lady is saying, shall we?"

Grace huffed, but folded her arms over her chest and fell silent.

"All we really know at this point is that it is some sort of enzyme, a hyaluronidase derivative of some sort. Hyaluronidase tends to break down the polysaccharides that hold cells together, and this particular variety seems to attack the bonds between endothelial cells. This causes all of the blood vessels to become porous, letting blood leak out into other areas of the body. Because the blood is saturated with hyaluronidase, it also works to break down the cellular matrix of other tissues, such as those around the eyes, nasal passages, auditory canals, the intestines and the urethra. That is how the blood manages to pass out of the body, but the effect is so extreme that blood would eventually begin leaking right through the skin." She made a face. "It's hard to say, but the patients may well be fortunate they don't live that long."

"So," Sam asked, "are you saying this is always going to be fatal?"

"Until we can identify the root cause, undoubtedly. We've tried every possible therapy we can think of, anything that is known to curtail the effects of hyaluronidase, but this one is not responding. Until we can identify its original chemical makeup, we don't know what to do."

Sam narrowed his eyes. "You said 'original chemical makeup,' just now. Are you implying that this is something that has been manipulated deliberately?"

Doctor Dione blinked. "Well, obviously, I can't say that for certain, but it's very difficult for me to believe an enzyme like this has developed naturally. A brand-new, undiscovered enzyme that could have effects like this would most likely be seen only in rare cases, not in a cluster the way these are happening. While I cannot say with absolute certainty that this is an artificial event, I will admit to being personally convinced that it must be. Someone is creating this enzyme, and then finding some way to introduce its effects into the victims. The only thing we are fairly certain of is that it isn't being delivered by injection; none of the victims seem to have had any kind of injections in the past few days. The only exception to that rule is one patient, Mr. Castiglione, who happens to be diabetic and takes insulin injections. We've tested his insulin and supplies, and there's no sign of the enzyme in any of them."

"Detective Garza has been looking at the possibility that all of the victims have something in common," Sam said, "but nothing seems to be connecting them. Have you observed anything that might shed some light on the subject?"

Dione looked at him for a moment, then shook her head. "These people come from all different backgrounds, we got representatives of all races, there's just nothing I can imagine that would be common to all of them. We even considered the possibility that this was a food-based vector, that perhaps they were all eating at the same place or something, but that didn't pan out, either."

Sam nodded. "That was a thought of my own, but it seems to be off track. We don't seem to have any leads on specific places they might have all been to, either."

"Well, what does that tell you?" Dione asked. "That indicates that, whatever the vector is, it can be found in more than one location. All of these people encountered it somewhere, but obviously not at the same place. That means there are multiple locations where it can be introduced into a victim."

Sam turned to Garza. "You and your officers have been talking to the families, right? Have you been able to nail down all the places these people might have gone in the day or so before they were affected?"

"Interviews are still going on," Garza said. "And every time there's a new victim, we have to start fresh with their families and friends. I hate to say it, but we're probably going to still be looking for common factors a week from now."

Sam shook his head. "We don't have a week," he said. "Somehow, we've got to find the source of this attack within the next twenty-four to forty-eight hours. I'm afraid that if we don't, it's going to spread a lot faster in the future, and it will almost certainly claim many more lives."

"I would have to concur," Dione said. "The first night we had less than a dozen victims, but by last night, we were well over forty. This morning we have a total of nearly eighty, so it's increasing exponentially. If we don't get a handle on it pretty soon, we will be looking at fatalities in the hundreds, and possibly up into the thousands."

Sam glanced around and noticed that none of the hospital personnel seemed to be wearing masks. He turned back to Dione. "I gather you don't think this is contagious?"

She shook her head. "The enzyme has to be introduced into the body. Basic precautions are all we need to avoid any of the staff getting infected with it. I can tell you that it isn't airborne, that's for certain. If it were, everyone who came within a few feet of a victim would be coming down with it. We are very lucky in that regard, because several of the first few victims came from very crowded environments, and nobody here stopped what they were doing to take precautions. Had it been airborne, we would probably be looking at a city-wide epidemic already."

Sam nodded. "I take your point," he said. "Have any of the victims been able to talk about what was happening to them?"

"No, I'm afraid not. By the time they get to us, they're basically comatose. The only signs of life are physiological; they don't respond to any stimulus at all."

"What causes that?" Sam asked.

"Well, blood loss. Blood that should be going to the brain is leaking throughout the entire body, so the cardiovascular system can't maintain sufficient blood pressure to get blood up into the brain. Without that, the brain shuts down to conserve what energy it has. In most of these cases, even if the patient were to survive, the brain damage would be so severe they'd probably need round-the-clock care for the rest of their lives. I doubt they would ever be able to speak or walk again; they certainly wouldn't be able to take care of themselves."

"Okay, let me ask this. From the time the infection becomes obvious, how long do you have to administer an effective treatment, if you find one?"

Dione twisted her face up and thought for a couple of seconds, then looked at Sam again.

"My best guess? An hour, ninety minutes at the most. After that, the brain damage is going to be severe and irreversible."

An alarm suddenly blared, and a voice came through the overhead speakers.

"Code blue, code blue. Doctor Dione, you are needed in exam room seventeen."

Dione turned without a word and hurried down the hall with Doctor Regalia following her. Sam and Garza were left standing where they were. They looked at one another, then started in the same direction.

"What does that mean, code blue?" Beauregard asked Grace.

Grace was looking down the hall toward where her son had just gone.

"It means somebody is dying," she said. "Right now."

Beauregard took her hand, and suddenly they were flying down the hall after the others.

"Come along, then," he said. "This may be the opportunity we've been waiting for."

"Opportunity?"

"Yes. If one of the victims passes away, we may have an opportunity to learn something from him before he's gone."

They arrived before Sam and Garza at the intensive care unit room where the code was called, and Grace stared at the people who were hurrying around the body that lay on the gurney. Beauregard, on the other hand, focused on the man who was standing off to the side, a look of confusion on his face.

"Hello, my friend," he said softly. "Do you understand what's happening?"

The man, who had been staring at the activity in the middle of the room, turned to look at him. "That's me, lying there," he said. "Am I dead?"

"I believe that to be the case, yes," Beauregard said. "I am sorry to bear such news, but I need to ask you some things while we can. Do you know what happened to you?"

The man looked blank and shrugged. "I have no idea," he said. "I was just sitting in my office a few minutes ago, or at least that's what I remember. Then all of a sudden I was here, watching those people trying to bring me back to life."

"Again, you have my sympathies. What I need to know, however, is if you have any idea how you became so ill. Can you tell me what you had done those last few hours?"

"What I did? I don't know, I left home this morning at the usual time. I stopped by the bank to get some cash out of the ATM, then went to Emilio's to grab a coffee. After that, I went to my office and started working, going over the files I was going to need later today." He blinked. "I'm an attorney—at least, I was an attorney." He looked at his body again, noting that the doctors were covering his face with a sheet. "What's going to happen now?"

Beauregard let out a sigh. "That will depend on you, I'm afraid. Most of us move on to whatever awaits us. You may see a light, or there may be a great darkness."

The man looked at Beauregard again. "Darkness? That doesn't sound good."

Grace gave a gasp and pointed toward the corner of the room, where a dark, swirling mist suddenly appeared. Beauregard and the late victim turned to look at it, and the man gave a cry as he was suddenly drawn into it. A second later, both the mist and the man were gone.

"Oh, my God," Grace said. "What happened to him?"

"I fear he was not a good man in this life," Beauregard said. "That is the fate that awaits those who have not made their peace with their maker." He turned to her, and then they both watched as the doctors filed out of the room. "I do wish that we could speak to Samuel," he said. "This Emilio's, he will want to know about that place. If other victims have also gone there, it could be where they are affected."

"If only we could," Grace said. "Maybe we should have made him bring Kim along. We could tell her, and she could tell him."

"Perhaps we will suggest that this evening," Beauregard replied. "Once Samuel knows that we can speak to the departed, perhaps he will find it a good idea."

The two of them followed Sam as he and Garza trailed behind Doctor Dione once again.

"When they go," Sam said, "I take it they go very quickly?"

"They do," she said. "The only blessing is that, by the time they get here, they can't really feel anything anymore. They don't suffer, so we can be grateful at least for that much."

"How long since he came in this morning?"

"He actually came in yesterday," Dione said. "He was at work when it hit him, and just suddenly collapsed. Paramedics brought him in, and we barely got him stable enough to move to the ICU. He actually lasted longer than some of the others we've had here."

Beauregard looked at Grace. "Interesting," he said. "The fellow could not remember anything of the time that he was ill. He thought only minutes had passed since he was at his duties."

Grace nodded. "Like the doctor said," she said. "That is the only blessing in any of this. They don't know just how bad off they are until it's over."

Sam turned to Detective Garza. "Ed, there has to be something we're missing. There has to be some common denominator between all of these people that we haven't found, and we have to find it."

"I agree, Sam," the detective replied. "I guess we just have to keep looking."

Beauregard scowled. "They need to know about this now," he said. He seemed to think for a moment, then gripped Grace's hand tightly. "Hold on," he said. "And pray that I know what I'm doing."

A second later, the two of them were rising from the floor and passing through the ceiling, continuing on through the upper floors of the hospital until they were in the open air. Grace gave another gasp as the world rushed by underneath them, even though there was no sensation of speed. From the way the ground was flying past below them, she couldn't even guess how fast they were going.

Only a few minutes later, they found themselves over the house the family lived in, and they settled right through the roof and to the first floor. They found Indie and Kim in the kitchen, while both children were in the living room, watching television. Without even stopping, they vanished and Kim's face suddenly registered surprise.

Indie stared at her for a second. "Mom? What is it?"

"It's Beauregard," she said, "and Grace. They said they have been with Sam this morning, and they need me to tell him something right away."

Indie's eyes narrowed. "Is it something bad?"

"No," Kim said, shaking her head. "They have some information that might help."

"Okay," Indie said. "I'll get him on the phone."

She took out her phone and dialed Sam's number, then put it on speaker so Kim could hear when he answered.

"Hey, babe," Sam said. "Everything okay back home?" There was stress in his voice, probably because he was thinking of Beauregard's warning.

"Everything okay at the moment," Indie said, "but Beauregard and your mom have a message for you."

"Sam," Kim said, "they've been gone all morning, and they just came back and told me they have been with you. Beauregard says they spoke to the man who died just a little while ago, and he told them that the only thing he did before he got sick that morning was stop for coffee at a place called Emilio's."

"Emilio's?" Sam repeated. They heard Garza in the background, saying something about it being a coffee shop downtown. "Wait a minute, they were here? They came with me this morning?"

Kim was nodding, even though Sam couldn't see her. "Yes, that's what they said. They went with you when you left, but Beauregard thought this was important enough for them to come back and have me call you."

"So, let me get this straight," Sam said. "They spoke to the ghost of the man who died?"

"Beauregard says that's absolutely right. Because they were there when he passed away, they were able to talk to him for a moment before he—before he moved on to his final destination."

Sam was silent for a couple of seconds. "Okay, then I guess I should say thank you, to you and to them. Ask them if they can come back to the hospital and talk to more of the victims that way."

Kim closed her eyes for a couple of seconds, then nodded. "He says he thinks they can, and they'll report back through me tonight. If they come upon something important, though, he says they will hurry back so I can call you again." She blinked. "Sam, they say you should take me with you. It would make all of this a lot faster, giving you information they find."

Sam hesitated, but then he cleared his throat. "I can't say that is a bad idea," he said, "but you do realize that puts you in danger, right? I mean, Beauregard has already warned us that someone in the family is going to be affected."

"I'm aware of that, Sam," Kim said, "but do you think I could live with myself if I can't do everything possible to help solve this case and put a stop to it? Beauregard has never been wrong, and he says somebody is deliberately killing people this way. That coffee shop might be part of it, but he wants to try to help more. In order to do that, at least to do it quickly enough that it could be important, he needs me to be close to you."

"Let's think about it, and we can talk about it tonight when I get home. For now, ask them to get back to the hospital. If anybody else dies, and they undoubtedly will, they might be able to give us something to go on." He suddenly chuckled. "I just hope I don't ever have to explain to the court how I got my information."

Indie took the phone back and took it off speaker. "Sam, just be careful down there. I am scared to death that you might be the one this is going to affect."

"I'll do my best," he said. "Meanwhile, maybe those two spooks can actually do us some good."

EIGHT

Garza looked at Sam as he hung up the phone. "Are you gonna tell me that was for real?"

Sam took a deep breath, then let it out in a huff. "I'm afraid it was. Listen, Ed, I know how crazy it sounds, but Beauregard is the real deal. He's an old Civil War ghost that somehow lives in my mother-in-law's head, but now he's roaming around and playing secret agent for us. I don't know about you, but I will take any help I can get on this case."

Garza's eyes were wide, but he was nodding his head. "I ain't laughing," he said. "Like I said, I read about Beauregard on your blog a couple years ago. I know a lot of people laugh about him, but I always had a hunch there was something true about it all." He shrugged. "My family came out of Mexico. You think we don't believe in ghosts? We celebrate them, remember? If you got a ghost who wants to help, I'm going to listen."

"Yeah," Sam said. "Me too. Now, where is Emilio's at? We need to go see if any of the other victims have been there."

"I can save you a little time," Garza said. "At least two other victims had been there for sure."

"Okay, we need to go get pictures of the victims and show them to the staff, there. See if they recognize anyone else."

"I'm ahead of you, got all their pictures on my phone already. Well, all the ones we had up to this morning, anyway. That should be enough to tell us if it is a popular place among the people who come down with this, right?"

"And what are we waiting for?" Sam asked. "Let's get moving."

They told Doctor Dione about the new lead and left the hospital immediately. Garza called Captain Harrison on his way out the door and filled him in, not bothering to mention the source of their information. He implied that it came from a relative of one of the victims, and Sam shot him a grateful look.

They got into the car and headed downtown once again, and it was almost twenty minutes later that they pulled in at a fancy-looking place with a sign that read "Emilio's." The two of them got out of the car again and walked inside, relieved to find the place almost empty at that moment. The young woman behind the counter smiled at them, but the smile disappeared when they flashed their IDs.

"I am Detective Garza with Orlando PD," Garza said. "This is Mr. Prichard, he's working with us on a very important case. Have you heard about the people who are getting sick all over the city?"

"Oh, yes," she said. "That is so terrible. I heard a lot of them have died already, is that true?"

"I'm afraid it is," Sam said. "We have just learned that some of the victims had stopped here for coffee a short time before they became sick. We were wondering if you might recognize any of the others."

Garza held out his phone and began sliding photos across the screen. "If you see anyone you recognize, stop me," he said. "This is very important, so please try to remember."

The girl leaned close and stared at the phone. Garza had gone through about a dozen photos when she said, "Stop. That guy, I know him. He comes in almost every day."

The picture she had chosen was the man who had just passed away a short time earlier. Garza thanked her, but asked her to keep looking at the other photos.

She picked out four more, but that was all she recognized. When they asked, she said that she was the normal day-shift barista, and had definitely been on duty the last four days straight.

"And nobody here has got sick?" Sam asked. "No one who works here?"

She shook her head. "No, not as far as I know. Nobody has called in sick or anything."

Sam turned to Garza. "Well, it was a lead," he said. "I think if this was the actual source of the illness, though, she would have recognized more people or some of the staff would be coming down with it."

"Yeah, I agree." Garza sighed. "Thank you anyway, miss," he said. "And please be careful. As far as we know, this is not actually contagious, but it is definitely coming from somewhere."

The girl nodded. "Yeah, for sure."

The two of them left the coffee shop and walked back toward the car.

"So," Sam said. "Any ideas on what to do next?"

"Me? Hey, you're the one who's supposed to be advising us, remember?"

"Don't remind me," Sam said. "I'm stressed out enough over this as it is. Beauregard warned me yesterday that some in my family are going to be affected by this—this whatever it is."

Garza's eyes went wide. "And he's, like, never wrong?"

Sam shook his head. "Unfortunately, never. That's why it is important we get to the bottom of this as quickly as we can. If that happens, I want Doctor Dione to be able to find an antidote or a treatment in time to save them."

Garza bit his bottom lip. "Let's go back to the station," he said. "Maybe if we go over all the victim files together, you'll see something I didn't."

"Worth a shot," Sam said. "We just have to keep at it until we find the answer."

Garza put the car in gear and the two of them went back to the police station. They sat down in the detective's office and began looking through the files on all of the victims. Each of the files contained general background information and a list of friends and family. Some of them had already been interviewed, but others had not. The two of them began making notes, planning to call each of those who had not yet been interviewed to see if they could get any kind of leads.

* * *

"I told you we should have followed the highways," Grace said. "It's not exactly like we can pull out a phone and turn on GPS."

She and Beauregard were hovering over what they were fairly sure was Orlando, but finding the hospital was turning out to be a problem.

"I suppose I should have paid more attention as we were leaving," he said morosely. "Can you think of any way we can find out where it is?"

"Not unless there's a ghost phone service," Grace shot back. "Then we could call information, or something."

Beauregard looked at her. "I don't know about that," he said, "but you've given me an idea."

He suddenly veered downward, and Grace had no choice but to go along. He settled onto a busy sidewalk and the two of them stood there for a moment as he looked around.

"There," he said after a moment. Grace looked in the direction he was pointing and saw a policeman standing on the corner.

"You're going to ask a cop? Aren't you going to be a little embarrassed when he can't hear you or see you?"

Beauregard grinned. "Look at his uniform," he said. "That doesn't look anything like the uniforms they were wearing at the police office this morning."

Grace looked, and then blinked. "You mean, he's a ghost?"

"I suspect he is." He held on to her hand and they walked along quickly, ignoring the people who did not get out of the way and simply passing through them. When he stopped in front of the policeman, the officer turned to look at them.

"Well," he said. "You've been hanging around a while, haven't you?"

"Sometimes it seems too long," Beauregard said. "However, I am in need of your assistance. Could you tell us how to get to the hospital?"

The policeman, who was wearing a name badge that said, "O'Flannery," raised his eyebrows. "Which one? There are several different hospitals in the city."

"It's Orlando Regional," Grace said. "A great big one."

"Oh, that's on Underwood. That's all the way across the city. Do you know your way around here?"

"I fear not," Beauregard said. "Would it be possible for you to show us the way?"

The policeman looked around behind himself for a moment, and they noticed he was looking at a sign that gave the time and temperature. He turned back a moment later with a smile.

"I have time," he said. "Just follow me."

He lifted off the ground and Beauregard took Grace's hand once more and followed. The city passed by underneath them all quickly, and it took only a matter of moments for them to arrive. The same hospital building they had left earlier loomed below them.

"Officer O'Flannery, you have my gratitude," Beauregard said.

The old cop looked at him. "Mind if I ask you something?" he asked. "As old as you are, you can't be waiting for someone to arrive in our state. What brings you to the hospital?"

"Actually," Beauregard said, "we are assisting your colleagues with an investigation. People seem to be dying of a strange illness, and we are attempting to help them learn what is causing it."

The ghostly officer's eyes went wide. "And are you for real? What can I do to help?"

Beauregard glanced at Grace, who nodded enthusiastically. He turned back to the officer.

"We are attempting to speak with those who pass away from this affliction," he said, "to ask if they can remember what they might have done that could have brought them in contact with it. This affliction happens quickly, within three hours after the person is infected. We have a way to communicate with someone who is working on the investigation, and he has asked us to speak with those who pass away, to see if we can find something they all have in common that might have exposed them to it." He looked at the eager face of the former policeman. "You could assist, if you wish."

"Sure, and it will be my pleasure!" O'Flannery said. "Shall we get to it, then?"

Without waiting for a reply, he dived into the building and vanished. Beauregard gave a *harrumph* and followed only a couple of seconds later.

Five more victims passed away that afternoon, and one of the three ghosts got to speak to each of them. None of them seemed to remember any great details about how they might have been affected, so they settled for asking what their last conscious hours were like.

Some of them went into great detail, talking about where they had had dinner, or what they had been doing at work before they fell ill, while others simply seemed confused.

"I don't know how I got here," one woman said. "I went to bed last night feeling fine; how did I end up here?"

"Can you tell us what you were doing the last few hours before you went to bed?" Grace asked softly. "Somehow, you got infected with this terrible illness. They say it works pretty fast, so we need to know what you were doing in the hours before it struck you."

The woman, who said her name was Margie, stared at her for a moment. "I don't know, I was out with some friends. We had gone out for a few drinks, went to a club, but that's about all I remember. Well, I remember getting home and getting into bed."

Beauregard rolled his eyes and they moved on. Another patient was crashing, so they wouldn't have long to wait before they could speak to another witness.

Officer O'Flannery was not having any better luck. He spoke with a number of people who were lingering around the hospital, having passed up the chance to move on into the light. Some of them had been there quite a while, but then he noticed a young black man in dreadlocks who seemed to be hovering around a crying older couple.

"Hello, lad," he said. "Would they be your parents?"

The young man turned to look at him. "Yeah," he said. "You a cop?"

"That I am. And it appears to me that you might be in need of some guidance?"

The young man—or more properly the boy, for he couldn't have been more than fifteen—glanced back at his parents, then turned to O'Flannery again. "I'm dead, right?"

"I'm afraid that's true," O'Flannery said. "What's your name, lad?"

"DeShawn," the boy said. "DeShawn Jackson."

"Well, DeShawn," O'Flannery said, "it seems there's something strange going 'round, and it is quite dreadful. From what I've learned, you seem to feel perfectly fine up until the moment it strikes, but then it takes you within hours. Can you recall what you might have been doing before it struck you?"

"You mean when I got dizzy, right? I got dizzy all of a sudden, and then I guess I blacked out. That what you mean?"

"Yes, that would be the onset. What might you have been doing the last few hours before that happened?"

DeShawn narrowed his eyes. "I was—I was just hanging with some friends. We been working on putting a band together, rap band, and we were working on some new lyrics. Me and Jamie, that's my girl, we stopped and picked up some pizza, so we all munched down on that, then we started working on the songs. Couple hours, I guess, and then all of a sudden I got dizzy. I remember Jamie asking me if I was okay, and then I—then I was here at the hospital, and there was doctors all over the place and stuff. I tried to talk to them, but they couldn't hear me, and then I saw my folks, they was standing in the doorway and Mama was crying."

He turned back toward his parents. "I've been trying to talk to them, but they can't hear me, neither. Can you talk to them? Can you tell them I'm okay?"

"I'm sorry, son," O'Flannery said. "I've never been able to get anyone to hear me, not since I passed away. It is all part of life, you know. We die, and those we leave behind, they grieve. There is naught you can do for them now. Only time will help them to heal."

DeShawn knelt down beside his mother and reached out as if to touch her, but his hand passed through her shoulder. She gave no sign that she felt anything.

"This ain't fair," he said. "This just ain't fair at all. I was going to be something, I was going to make something out of myself. What I am supposed to do now?"

O'Flannery pursed his lips. "Have you seen the light yet, son?"

DeShawn looked up at him. "The light? What you talking about? You mean, like, did I get religion?"

"When we die, where we go next is determined by what we see. If you see a bright light, that is a sort of invitation, to step on into heaven, I suppose. Have you seen one?"

DeShawn shook his head. "I ain't seen nothing, yet, except all this." He hesitated for a second or two. "If I don't see the light, does that mean I'm going the other way?"

"I think not," O'Flannery said. "For those who are headed down that path, there is a darkness that appears, and they are drawn to it irresistibly. That usually happens quickly, though. The light, it comes when you are ready for it, I think. It seems to give us time to consider what we are leaving behind."

"Didn't you see a light?"

"Aye, I did," O'Flannery said honestly. "I chose to stay, though. I had a young son when I died, and I decided to stay and watch him grow up."

DeShawn nodded. "I guess I could understand that," he said. "You think maybe I could stay, and kind of watch over my folks?"

O'Flannery looked at him for a moment, then glanced at his parents, who were still weeping over the loss of their son.

"And do you think that would be what they would want you to do? If you move on, perhaps there is a band waiting for you. If you stay here, you will only watch them suffer with their grief, and there will be nothing you can do for them."

DeShawn looked at him for a moment longer, then turned back to his parents. "I'll keep an eye out for the light," he said over his shoulder.

O'Flannery laid a hand on the boy's shoulder and squeezed it gently. "I think that is best," he said.

He turned away and continued looking for more of the victims, but there did not seem to be many of them lingering. He spotted Beauregard and Grace at the other end of the hall and floated toward them.

"Are you having any luck?" he asked.

Beauregard shook his head. "We don't seem to be finding anything that all of them had in common," he said. "They talk about going out for dinner, or for drinks, or doing the shopping, but they all seem to have gone to different places."

"Agreed," O'Flannery said. "I spoke to one who works at a bank, but she has no idea what could've happened to her. Another, a teenage boy, told me about buying pizza and making music with his friends in his final hours. Nothing seems to be connecting them all together."

"Then maybe the problem is that it is happening in lots of different places," Grace said. "Maybe this is coming from a hundred different places, not just one."

O'Flannery shook his head. "If that were true, madam, there would be hundreds or thousands of victims, not the dozens we see. For that many places to become infected would mean a greater number of people would fall to this affliction."

Beauregard seemed to chew the inside of his cheek. "I see the sense in what you say," he said. "So, then, there is something we are failing to recognize. Something that all of them have done or come in contact with. What we have to determine is what it could be, but that may be beyond our abilities."

"Then share what we have learned with your investigator," O'Flannery said. "If God be willing, perhaps he will see a pattern that escapes us."

NINE

Sam hung up the phone for the twentieth time and looked across the desk at Garza.

"Same old story," he said. "That was the sister of a man who died yesterday. The only thing she knows about what he was doing his last few hours was that he met her for lunch, then went back to work and collapsed a couple hours later. He worked at a hardware store, but nobody else around him came down with it, so I don't think he encountered it there."

"I'm getting the same stuff," Garza said. "People going about their normal lives, nothing out of the ordinary at all. My last one was the widow of a man who stopped and picked up doughnuts for his office, then spent the morning in a meeting. He was talking with his sales team about business when he suddenly just fell over, and they saw the blood in his eyes. All of his activities were perfectly normal for him, it is the kind of thing he did every day."

Sam glanced at the clock on the wall and saw that it was after four. "Well, we can hope our secret agents had better luck. I'm going to head for home, Ed, but if they have anything interesting, I'll give you a call."

Garza nodded. "I'd appreciate that," he said. "I'll see you in the morning?"

"Yes," Sam said. "I'll be here around seven, just like this morning. Maybe tomorrow will be better and we'll actually get somewhere on this thing."

"I hope so. The captain texted me a bit ago, says there's been another thirty victims come in."

Sam shook his head and got to his feet. "I feel bad going home," he said. "If I thought there was anything we could learn by staying, I would, but Beauregard and my mother may be our best hope. I'll call you if I find out anything good, and I'll see you in the morning no matter what."

The two men shook hands and Sam walked out of the office. He made his way through the building and out to the parking lot, climbed into his Mustang and started the big engine. He let it idle out of the parking lot and then accelerated into the traffic on the street.

During the drive home, he concentrated on going over all of the things he had heard. Each of the victims had been doing something perfectly normal, with the exception of one who had recently robbed someone at gunpoint. No one was hurt, thank God, but the man got away with a few hundred dollars that his victim had just pulled out of the ATM. Other than that one, all of the victims had been going about their normal, daily lives. If there was anything linking them together, Sam had yet to spot it.

About halfway home, he took out his phone and called Indie. "Hey, babe," he said. "Any sign of our wandering spooks yet?"

"Not yet," she said. "Mom and I are making dinner, but they haven't turned up since they left. Any idea when you are going to be home?"

"About half an hour," Sam said. "I'm on the way now. I was hoping they might have come back and had something to report."

"Well, if they had," she said, "I'm sure we would have called you.

Knowing Beauregard, he would've been insisting on it if he thought he had anything that might help."

Sam chuckled. "Good point," he said. "So, what's for dinner?"

"I put a roast in the oven a couple hours ago, so we are working on making mac and cheese and homemade biscuits to go with it. It should all be ready by the time you get here."

"Good," Sam replied. "All I had for lunch was a sandwich out of a machine, so I could stand an early dinner. Kids okay?"

"They're fine. Kenzie has Bo out on the deck, playing with Samson. They've got him chasing something on the end of a string, and Bo is laughing his butt off."

Sam grinned. "As long as Samson doesn't try to run too fast," he said. "He always ends up in a tumble when his back legs pass up his front legs." Samson had survived a bout with distemper when he was young, but it had left him with some neurological damage. While most cats were graceful, Samson was notoriously clumsy.

They said their goodbyes, whispered a few sweet words to one another, and then Sam ended the call. He arrived home just as the roast was coming out of the oven and spent a few minutes playing with the kids and the cat before they were called to the table.

Dinner was over and they were all sitting comfortably in the living room almost an hour and a half later when Kim's face suddenly lit up. "They're back," she said.

Sam looked at her. "Mom and Beauregard?"

Kim nodded. "Yes, give me a minute," she said. "Beauregard is trying to tell me everything in a hurry. Beauregard, slow down, please."

She closed her eyes and sat there for a moment, then let out a sigh. A couple of seconds later, her face underwent the familiar transformation, relaxing from its normally smiling countenance to one of stoic calm.

Her eyes opened and she looked at Sam. "Hello, Samuel," she said, her voice somehow deeper and more masculine.

Sam let out a sigh of his own. "Hello, Beauregard."

"I felt it better to deliver my report personally," Kim/Beauregard said. "I am sorry to say that I do not have any wonderful news to give you, but I hope you will be able to make more of it than I could."

Beauregard, speaking through Kim, proceeded to give Sam a detailed report of the conversations he, Grace and Officer O'Flannery had had at the hospital. He carefully included every detail he could remember, and Sam picked up a pen and paper and took notes. When he was finished, he looked at Sam again.

"I hope you have considered my suggestion, that Ms. Kimberly be permitted to go along tomorrow. If an opportunity arises to learn something of importance, it would be best if we could relay it to you immediately, don't you think?"

"I've been thinking about that," Sam said. "On the other hand, you are the one who said some of my family are going to be affected by this thing. How do I know it won't be Kim, if I take her along?"

"I wish I knew more, but I don't. My forebodings do not come with details most of the time, so I don't have any way to tell you whether it will put her at greater risk or not. Obviously, the greatest danger seems to be in Orlando, but you must decide if the potential benefit is worth that risk."

Sam bit his bottom lip for a moment, then nodded. "I understand that it makes sense, so I'll go along with it as long as Kim is willing. It's got to be her call."

"Of course," Beauregard said. "And now, I shall let her speak for herself."

Kim's head drooped forward for a second, then snapped back up and she blinked. "Okay, I'm back," she said. "And yes, Sam, I am more than willing. If I can be of any kind of help at all, I want to."

Sam looked down at his notes. There was nothing there that he hadn't already heard from many other people, and yet he had the nagging feeling he was missing an important clue that was right before him. He read through the notes again, then set them aside. Perhaps if he looked at them later, with his eyes and mind fresh from a healthy distraction, it might jump out at him.

The television was on and they returned to the program they had been watching. It was a comedy about a woman who was pretending to be a man in order to get and keep the job she wanted, and both Kim and Indie thought it was delightful. Sam found it bearable, and even managed to chuckle at some of the antics the star got up to from time to time.

The show ended, and Sam switched to a news channel. It was an Orlando station, and the host of the program who was on was talking about the illness that was ravaging victims in the city.

"I've been told by a representative of the CDC that this is not a normal epidemic of any kind," he was saying. "On the contrary, it appears that this is some sort of manufactured disease, possibly even a biological terror attack. We've been fortunate so far that every appearance has been here in Orlando, because it means that the attack is isolated to this area for the moment, but now things are changing. We now have two reports of the same symptoms appearing in other Florida communities. One case is in Lake City, up near the Florida-Georgia line, and the other is in Fort Myers. Neither of the victims has been to Orlando lately, so authorities are rushing to try to figure out how the disease is appearing in these locations."

Indie turned to Sam, her face ashen. "It's spreading out," she said. "Sam, this is frightening."

"I agree," Sam said. "If it's turning up in other cities, then whoever is behind it has been pretty busy."

"Daddy," Kenzie said suddenly. "Are people here going to get sick with that?"

Sam looked at his daughter. "We hope not, sweetheart," he said. "The trouble is, we don't know yet what's causing it. It could come here, but I'm going to do everything I can to keep that from happening."

Sam took out his phone to call Garza, but it rang before he got a chance and he saw that it was the detective, calling him.

"Prichard," he said.

"Sam, it's Ed. I just got the word, cases of this are popping up in different places around the state."

"Yes, I just heard that myself. Lake City and Fort Myers."

"That's not all," Garza said. "There are now three cases in Jacksonville, and more than a dozen in Miami. Whoever is doing this, Sam, they're stepping up their game."

Sam nodded into the phone. "I agree," he said. "That means that Orlando was probably just a test run. Whoever it is wanted to see just how effective it would be in the city environment."

"Yeah. So, did the, uh, special agents come up with anything?"

"They got a lot of the same things we heard today. I took notes, and I'm going to look at them again in a while to see if anything jumps out at me, but so far, I feel like we're just missing something, and it's probably something pretty important."

"Yeah, I feel the same way. It's like, I know what I'm looking for is there, but I can't see it. Forest hidden by the trees, right?"

"That's how it feels, yes. Has anyone made contact with the police in those other cities yet?"

"I doubt it, we just started hearing about this. Only reason I know about it tonight is because I left word for any new developments connected to this case to be sent to me immediately. I figure we can contact them tomorrow and see what they know, but right now, I would guess that we are out ahead of them."

"That is pretty sad, considering we don't really know anything."

Sam rubbed a hand over his face. "All right, Ed, I'll see you in the morning unless something new comes up."

"See you, Sam." The line went dead.

Indie was watching his face, so he turned toward her. "Miami and Jacksonville," he whispered. "Multiple cases."

She swallowed hard. "Jacksonville isn't that far away," she said.

"No, but it isn't next door, either. Don't lose hope, babe."

"I'm not, Sam. I just can't help thinking about what Beauregard said."

They went back to watching television again, switching to a comedy movie to lighten the mood. After a few minutes, they even managed to laugh, and Sam felt himself relaxing. He let himself go into that feeling, putting Orlando and the case out of his mind the best he could.

When the movie was over, Indie went to put Bo to bed for the night while Kenzie and Kim decided to play a game at the kitchen table. Sam reached over and picked up the notes he had made and began reading through them once again.

Still, it looked a lot like the notes he had taken during the day from the police station. Each of the victims reported doing only normal things in the last few hours before the condition struck. Sam couldn't see any particular things that seemed to be repeated, so he decided to make a simple comparison chart. Taking a separate sheet of paper, he began listing particular points from each person's story, one line at a time. Some of the people had been at home, so he put "home" on one line. Some had gone out for dinner, so he put "out to eat" on the line, followed by "out drinking" for those who had said they were doing so. Some of the people had mentioned where they had gone, but none of them matched up, so he did not bother to list the individual places.

Some had fallen sick at work, so he put "work" on a line. Some had done so in bed, asleep, so he put "bed" on a line. Some had eaten pizza, so "pizza" got listed. On another line, he put "chicken" and followed that up with "burgers." For those who had brought dinner home, he wrote "takeout."

When he was finished, he had twenty lines with a single word on each. With that as a reference, he went back through each story and put a checkmark by each of the words that appeared in that story. Since two of the interviewed ghosts had been at home the last they remembered, he had two checkmarks beside the word "home."

When he had finished checking them off, he looked at the list again. There were two checkmarks beside "home," six checkmarks beside "out to eat," and three checkmarks beside "pizza." "Work" had five checkmarks, and "out drinking" had three. "Bank" had three checkmarks, and "ATM" had two. "Takeout" had three checkmarks of its own.

Looking at the columns of checkmarks, he tried to think of what all of these things might have in common. What could being at home, for example, have in common with going out to eat, or going out drinking? He couldn't think of a sensible answer to that question, so he moved on.

What did going out to eat have in common with going out drinking? Well, obviously, they were not at home, that was one thing. They would take place in a public location, most likely, so that was two common factors. The victim probably was not alone, so that was a third.

What did either of those have in common with pizza? Well, you could eat pizza by going out to eat, and were probably not alone when you did so. You could also eat pizza if you took it home, so that possibly connected it to those who brought dinner home.

Sam started to think he might be on to something, even if he did not yet know what it was. Something about analyzing the information this way was giving him a hopeful feeling. He decided to keep going.

Now, what could takeout have in common with going to the bank or the ATM? Quick and simple answer, in order to pick up dinner, you had to have money. Of course, that applied to everything else on the list, with the possible exception of just sitting at home. You had to have money to go out drinking, to go out to eat, to pick up dinner or get pizza…

Common denominator, Sam thought. I just found the common denominator. Each and every one of these people almost certainly handled money in those last few hours before the symptoms became obvious.

Of course, some of them could have used credit or debit cards, and there were even apps for your phone, now, that you could use to pay for things. Still, Sam thought he was on to something. If all of these people had paid in cash, then that was a definite common denominator between them all.

He glanced at his phone for the time and saw that it was still a few minutes shy of ten p.m., so he dialed Garza's number. "Ed, I think I found something," he said as soon as the detective answered. "The only thing I can find that all of these people had to have had in common was that they almost all likely handled money in the hours before they got sick."

"Money? What, you mean like cash?"

"I think so," Sam said. "Some of the people had been to the ATM, and some had been to the bank. Almost all of them did something that required spending money in that last few hours, either going out to eat, buying something, whatever. It's the only thing I can find that all of them seem to have in common."

"So, you are thinking maybe something happened to them at the bank? Or at the ATM?"

"You're getting ahead of me, Ed," Sam said. "I haven't figured out how this is connected to the infection, yet, but I think it is. Something about handling money is connected to what's going on. I'm telling you, I can feel it in my gut."

"Yeah, and mine is saying your gut is right. We just have to figure out how it fits in. You want to keep on this tonight, or should we wait and talk about it in the morning?"

"I think we need to start on this in the morning," Sam replied. "I just felt like I should tell you about it now, so we can both sleep on it. Maybe one of us will come up with something new by morning."

"Okay, yeah, that makes sense. All right, Sam, I'll see you in the morning."

Sam cut off the call and set the phone on the table beside his chair, then noticed Indie standing beside him.

"You found something?" she asked.

"Maybe," he said. "I was going over the notes I took from what Beauregard said, and it dawned on me that almost everybody, including the people Ed and I checked out today, probably used money not long before they got sick. I haven't figured out how that fits in, but I think it is something about the money."

Indie's eyebrows rose slightly. "Like, maybe, something on the money itself? Something that rubs off on them?"

"I hadn't gotten that far, but that's not an unreasonable thought. We know it acts like an infection, even if it is something that was made in a laboratory. I suppose it's quite possible it is something that can be absorbed through touch."

TEN

Morning came, and Sam got up to find the coffee already hot and waiting. Kim was sitting at the table, a cup of coffee in front of her as he poured his own.

"You sure you want to do this?" he asked. "We may have some ideas on what's going on, so it may not be necessary at all. You could be putting yourself in danger for no reason, Kim."

"I don't see what it could hurt for me to ride along," she said. "I mean, I'm only there in case Beauregard needs to tell you something, right? I can just stay back out of the way."

Sam took a sip from his coffee and shook his head. "Okay, it's your call. I just don't want to be the cause of Beauregard's prediction coming true, you know what I mean? If you come down with this, Indie's never going to forgive me."

"Yes, she will," Kim said. "We talked about this, Sam. She knows this is my choice, and she says she completely understands why I want to do it. If Beauregard or your mother could talk directly to you, then you wouldn't need me; as it is, maybe I can be useful for once."

"Do not ever," Sam said emphatically, "ever think of yourself as not useful. I don't how many times you've come to the rescue when Indie and I just needed a break from the kids, and you've taught both of us a lot about what raising kids really means."

"Thank you," Kim replied modestly, "but I've made my share of mistakes, too, Sam. I don't know if Indie ever told you, but—well, I just was not always the best mother. I had a boyfriend once, and Indie tried to tell me he was acting out of line with her, but I wouldn't listen. It got to the point that she moved out because I wouldn't get rid of him, and then it was a few weeks later when I learned the truth." She sighed. "I honestly thought she was saying it just because she was jealous, that I wasn't paying her enough attention or something. I should have listened. Because of me, she and Kenzie ended up homeless."

Sam sat there in silence for a few seconds. "I know that story," he said finally. "Indie told me. Of course, that was the reason she was homeless when I met her. If she hadn't been, if she hadn't been desperate at the time, she might never have given me a second glance. As it was, we found each other because of that, and I think you can agree that it worked out for the best. Don't beat yourself up over it, Kim. Humans make mistakes, and we are all human."

Kim suddenly giggled. "Beauregard said he resents that comment," she said. "He says he gave up humanity a long time ago."

"Baloney, and you can tell him I said that," Sam said. "If he wasn't human, he wouldn't have that bad a sense of humor."

They finished the coffee and each of them made it to take along, then headed out toward the Mustang. They got into the car and Sam backed out of the driveway, then gave the big engine its head as he pointed it toward Orlando.

"Are they with us?" he asked as they pulled away.

"They're here," Kim said. "I can hear Beauregard talking to your mother."

"But you can't hear Mom?"

Kim shook her head. "No, not directly. I don't know why for sure, but Beauregard is the only one I can hear. If your mom wants to tell me something, she tells Beauregard and he relays it to me."

Sam shook his own head in sympathy. "I don't know how you deal with it," he said. "I don't think I could cope with people living inside my head, even if they were dead."

"It's not that bad, once you get used to it. When I first met Beauregard, I actually thought I was going crazy. We were living in this little shack in Kentucky, and I would hear this voice telling me things. At first, I thought it was just my imagination, but then some of the things he told me kept Indie from getting hurt, so I started to believe it. When I started asking questions, that's when he told me who he was." She grinned. "And then, of course, we found out he was one of my ancestors. I guess it really is a small world in some ways, right?"

"Maybe that's the reason you can hear him," Sam said. "Maybe it is some kind of family connection?"

"Possibly. I vaguely remember stories about my grandmother having some kind of special ability, but I don't know if it was talking to dead people or not."

Sam gave a shudder. "I'm still glad I don't have to deal with it myself. The thought of Mom being in my head, knowing everything I do…"

"Yes," Kim said, giggling again. "It does get a little embarrassing, sometimes. When I had a boyfriend, for example, I had to take Beauregard's word for it that he was not paying attention when I asked for privacy. I mean, how could I know for sure?"

"Wow," Sam said. "I never even thought about things like that. I guess it takes the concept of intimacy to a whole different level, doesn't it?"

"I think you are beginning to catch on," Kim said. "But, like I said, you get used to it after a while. Then it's not that big a deal, anymore."

"Fine, but it can be your deal. I'll be happy to stay out of that one."

The conversation went on in a similar vein until they arrived in Orlando, and Sam was delighted to see that Garza had picked up some doughnuts for them on his way into the office. When he looked at them, however, he remembered the lady who said her husband had picked up doughnuts as one of the last things he ever did, and suddenly lost his appetite.

He settled for coffee and quickly reintroduced Kim to the detective. Garza looked at her for a moment and then found an extra chair for her to sit in while he and Sam sat down.

"You're the lady who can talk to the ghosts, right?" Garza asked when they were all seated.

"Just one," Kim said. "The only one I can talk to or hear is Beauregard. I know that there is another one, Sam's mother, but I can't actually hear her or talk to her." She blinked. "Okay, Beauregard says I can talk to her because she can hear everything I say, but I can't hear her responses. He has to relay those to me."

The detective stared at her for a few seconds. "You know how crazy everybody would think I was if I told them about you? And yet, I am absolutely convinced you are telling the truth."

"You'd better be," Sam said. "It was Beauregard and Mom who got us enough information to set us on the right path."

Garza turned to him. "I'm not complaining," he said. "I am just saying. If I went out and told everybody else in this building I had a lady here who could talk to a ghost, they would start wondering if I needed a vacation. Or rehab."

Sam chuckled. "Now you know how I've been feeling for the past few years."

"I've been here since about six," Garza said, changing the subject, "and I started looking at all the notes we have on the victims we've checked so far. Sam, you may be on to something, because almost every one of them made some kind of purchase within that last few hours. I decided to check out their finances, and I've been going over things like credit and debit card purchases. Want to know the interesting thing I found out?"

"Let me guess," Sam said. "These folks do not have credit cards, and they do not like using debit cards all the time."

"Pretty close," Garza said. "Most of them do not have credit cards, you were right about that, but most of them also do not have a regular debit card. All they have is an ATM card. With those, you can't use them to pay for something at the store, you have to get the cash out of the machine first."

"You mean those still exist? I figured by now, everybody would be using regular debit cards of some kind. I think my daughter has one, and she is only going on eight years old. Of course, her mother keeps it, but we opened a bank account for her a while back and I am sure they gave her a debit card."

"Yeah, even savings accounts get them, now. I guess it's because of that whole 'cashless society' idea, how we're slowly moving toward not having cash at all anymore."

"Yeah," Sam mused. "So, these people did not have any plastic they could use to pay for dinner or pizza or drinks or whatever, right? They had to use cash. Last night, when I was talking to my wife about this, she made the comment that it could be something that is actually on the money, something that rubs off on the skin and maybe that is how it's affecting people."

"I think that makes a lot of sense," Garza said. "What do you say we go talk to Dione about that? She could probably tell us if that is really possible, don't you think?"

"If anybody can," Sam said. "Sure, let's go."

Kim looked up at him. "Should I come along?"

"Absolutely," Sam said. "Now that we know what to ask about, Beauregard and Mom can interview a few more of the victims."

* * *

They arrived at the hospital a short time later and Sam asked Kim to simply have a seat in the waiting area. She found a coffee machine and got a cup, then sat down while Sam and Garza went looking for Doctor Dione.

"I miss coffee," Grace said. "Don't you ever wish we could have a cup of coffee, or bite into a sandwich?"

One of Beauregard's eyebrows went up slightly. "I remember a time when I did have such ideas," he said, "but that faded away long ago." They were standing beside Kim, and he looked down at her. "Strangely enough, I can still remember what coffee tasted like."

"Yes, so can I, and I am craving a cup. Oh, never mind, let's go find something to help Sam."

The two of them walked down the hall toward the ER, and it did not take them long to find the first disembodied spirit. It was a woman, and she was standing in the hallway, looking confused.

"Hello," Grace said to her. "Are you okay?"

The woman stared at her for a moment. "Oh, you can see me?"

"Yes," Grace said, nodding. "Do you understand what's happening?"

The woman looked around for a moment, turning back to look into one of the examination rooms where a number of people were standing around a sheet-covered body.

"I think so," she said as she turned back to them. "I think I'm dead. Am I dead?"

"I'm afraid so, dear," Grace said. "Do you know what happened to you?"

"Damn right I do," the woman said. "That bastard husband of

mine wrecked the damn car! Ran head-on into a semitruck, he did."

Grace looked at Beauregard, her eyes wide. Beauregard stepped forward to take over the conversation.

"Madam, are you saying you died in a simple accident?"

"I don't know if it was an accident or not," she said. "We just left home a while ago to go on vacation, we were going out to Colorado to see the kids. Jim, he went out this morning and gassed up the car, picked up some stuff for us to snack on during the trip, and then came back and helped me load everything up. He had to make a stop in the can, you know, and then when he finally came out of there, we got in the car and headed out. We just got on the highway when he swerved over in the wrong lane, and I looked at him and, good God, he had blood running down his face. Looked like he was crying blood, you know what I mean? Next thing I know, I heard this loud horn and looked up and we done cut across the median into the other lane, big old semitruck coming right at us!" She glanced around at where her body lay once again, then turned back to Beauregard. "I guess I didn't make it. I was getting ready to try to find Jim, see if he's okay, but I don't know where to go."

Beauregard cleared his throat. "You do indeed have a firm grasp of the situation," he said. "Now, you said that he looked like he was crying blood. There was blood coming from his eyes?"

"Damn right there was," she said. "And I mean a lot of it! Good God, I never saw any such a thing!"

"I see. Now, can you tell me, how long was he gone to run those errands this morning? Was it a few hours?"

"Oh, couple hours, I guess. He went down to the 7-Eleven, he likes to flirt with that girl behind the counter down there. He said he got gas and picked up some candy and chips and stuff, then grabbed us some doughnuts and came back, but that shouldn't take two hours, should it? I know darn well he was down there checking her out, whether he wants to admit it or not."

Beauregard turned to Grace, his eyes asking her to step in and intervene. She took pity on him.

"Would he have paid for everything with a credit card?" Grace asked.

"Credit card? Nah, Jim didn't have no use for things like that. He woulda used the ATM there at the 7-Eleven, got out enough money for the trip and stuffed it all down in a pocket."

"Cynthia?" a man's voice called out, and the woman suddenly spun to look in the direction it had come from. "Cynthia, are you all right?"

"Am I all right? Hell, no, I'm not all right, you killed us, you stupid idiot! What the heck did you think, cutting into the other lane like that? We went head-on into a big rig, you imbecile!"

The man who had spoken to her, whom Beauregard and Grace assumed was her husband Jim, came toward them. He seemed to do a double take when a couple of people stepped right through him, and his eyes betrayed the shock he appeared to be feeling.

"But how did that happen?" he asked. "I was just driving along, and then I kinda woke up here. What on Earth happened?"

"I told you," Cynthia said, "you killed us, you big..."

"Okay, hold on," Grace said. "Cynthia, this isn't his fault. You know that thing about the blood coming out of his eyes? Have you heard about people getting sick all of a sudden and dying around here? Well, that is one of the symptoms. Once that starts, the person usually loses consciousness and can't remember anything after that."

"I don't care, it's still his fault," Cynthia said. "If he hadn't been down there ogling that girl, maybe we would have been somewhere else and wouldn't have hit that truck! I was wearing a seat belt, I might have lived through it if we just had a regular accident."

She turned back to her husband and started berating him again, and Beauregard took hold of Grace's arm to lead her away. They hadn't gone far when they spotted a young man who walked right through a wall in front of them.

"Excuse me," Beauregard said. "Have you been here very long?"

The fellow looked around at him. "Oh, hi," he said. "No, just a few hours, I guess. I'm dead. Since you can talk to me, I guess you must be dead, too. Right?"

"Indeed," Beauregard replied. "Would you happen to know how you came to be in this condition?"

"You mean how I croaked?" The young man grinned. "All I know is I was at work, and I started feeling really weird, and then I woke up here a while ago. It was really freaky, you know? I actually got to see them trying to bring me back to life, but then they pulled the sheet up over my face and that was that."

"I see. Can I ask where you were working?"

"Oh, sure. It was Gallagher's Pizza, down on Palm Bay. Must've been last night, I guess, because when I started to realize what was happening, it was daytime again."

Beauregard looked at him for a moment, and then leaned a little closer. "Would you remember if a young fellow, a young black man, came in to buy some of your pizza? He had very long hair, all twisted up."

Another grin spread across the fellow's face. "Oh, you mean DeShawn? Yeah, he comes in a couple times a week. He's a good kid, got a lot of talent, too."

Beauregard nodded. "And he paid you with cash money?"

"Well, yeah, he always does. Why? Something unusual about that?"

Beauregard turned to Grace. "I believe we need to get back to Miss Kimberly," he said. "I think we have just confirmed what Samuel believes."

ELEVEN

Sam and Garza had gone to find Doctor Dione and caught up with her at the ICU nurses' station. She looked up as they approached and tried to smile, but the exhaustion in her eyes kept it from spreading across her face properly.

"Detectives," she said. "I'm afraid I don't have anything new to tell you."

"Understood," Sam said. "But we think we may have a lead on how people were coming into contact with whatever is causing this. We were going over all the different things that we knew people had done in the last few hours before they got so sick and found only one thing that they all seemed to do. Every single one of them, as far as we can tell, handled money. Almost all of them either don't have a credit card or won't use them for one reason or another, and were using cash, instead. That makes us wonder if there could be something on the money that is causing this. Can you think of anything that might do that?"

"On the money?" she asked, her eyes narrowed. "It would have to be something that could pass through the skin of the fingers, but that wouldn't be terribly difficult. The addition of DMSO would help to facilitate that transmission, letting whatever substance is used be absorbed directly through the skin and into the blood." She pursed her lips and thought for a moment, then her eyes opened wide. "Micro RNA molecules," she said. "Mir-105-C is a synthetic replica of a natural enzyme that has the capability of destroying the cellular integrity of endothelial cells, and it is far more potent than the natural variety. Natural Mir-105 is normally found in patients with pancreatic cancer, but this version can be synthesized in the laboratory, and it wouldn't take much to be able to work its way through the entire vascular system and do its damage. In pancreatic cancer, it breaks down endothelial cells in order to allow cancer cells to pass through the vascular wall, resulting in metastasis, the spread of the cancer to other organs. This version, once it entered the bloodstream, would take less than a minute to reach the heart, and then maybe another five minutes for it to be distributed throughout the body. It will start degradation as soon as it comes into contact with endothelial cells in each part of the circulatory system, so within two and a half to three hours, it would have reached the point of maximum permeability. The entire circulatory system would be leaking everywhere by that point, resulting in the symptoms we've seen."

Sam and Garza glanced at one another, then Sam turned back to the doctor. "So, you're saying that it could be transmitted simply by touching money that has been impregnated with it?"

"Damn right," Doctor Dione said. "But, does that really make sense? Wouldn't everybody who touches that money be affected?"

"You would certainly think so," Sam said. "On the other hand, we don't know how much money has been treated this way. Some people have gotten money from an ATM, we know that much, so that means the perpetrator has some way of getting it into the banks. It gets put into the ATM in stacks, usually, so maybe nobody touches it until it is actually dispensed. That's what we need to find out next."

The conversation went on for a while, and the three of them

discussed the many ways tainted money can get into people's hands. It would not only be dispensed through ATMs, but could also be received in change while making purchases, and of course there was the fact that handing money to a cashier would likely transmit the effect to that cashier, as well.

"Sam," Kim called out, and they turned to see her coming up the hallway. "I have something for you."

Sam caught the look in her eye that meant she wanted to talk privately, and he left Detective Garza with the doctor as he stepped into a quiet room that was normally used for doctors to confer with families of patients.

"Okay, what is it?" Sam asked.

Kim licked her lips and looked him in the eye. "Beauregard says they have been talking to some of the latest victims. There was a couple who died in a car accident when the husband suddenly got this sickness while he was driving, and the young man who worked at the pizza place where another victim bought pizza a couple of nights ago. He apparently got it when the money was handed over for the pizza. That proves what you were thinking, right?"

Sam nodded. "Yes," he said. "That pretty well confirms the conclusion we'd already come to. Tell them I said thanks—never mind, they can hear me. Beauregard, Mom, thank you. Now, if we can find out where people are getting the money, that might help us track down who's behind it."

Kim's eyes bobbed around for a couple of seconds, then she grinned. "They said they'll get on that right now," she said. "Sam, this is kind of exciting, being here to help like this."

"Don't get too excited," Sam said with a grin. "And whatever you do, do not touch any money."

Kim went back toward the waiting room while Sam returned to Garza and the doctor. The detective looked at him curiously, but

Sam shook his head, almost imperceptibly.

"She came up with something that kinda confirms our suspicions," he said carefully. "I think we need to start working on how this tainted money is getting into circulation, and work backwards from there. In order to do that, though, we're probably going to have to start testing the money itself. Doctor Dione, how can we do that?"

Dione looked at him for a couple of seconds, then shrugged. "I would normally say to bring it to a lab for testing," she said, "but you don't have time for that. You find money you want to test, you call me and I will send a couple of our bright techs to you. They'll need to look for Mir-105-C, probably mixed with dimethyl sulfoxide. The money will most likely feel oily, but you don't want to get it on your fingers. This stuff is going to work fast, since it is going directly into the bloodstream."

"How long before you can confirm this is the stuff that's causing it?" Sam asked. "And is that going to lead to any kind of treatment?"

"I've already ordered tests on the blood samples we have, and we should have results back within half an hour. The lab techs we brought along from the CDC are very good, and they know their jobs. As for treatment—yes, I can think of a couple of possible ways to counteract the effects. I won't know how effective they are until we actually try them, though, and I don't dare attempt to use them until we are certain we have the right cause."

Garza shook his head. "Why not? I mean, as it is right now, these people are going to die, right? Why can't you try the treatments you are thinking of; it certainly can't make matters worse, can it?"

"Yes, it could," Dione said scornfully. "The particular things I am thinking of, such as cisplatin, can have some pretty serious side effects and might even make the condition worse if we happen to be wrong about what's causing it. I am not going to take a chance on something that could make these people's lives even shorter than they already are."

Garza looked slightly abashed, but Sam nodded. "Of course, we understand," he said. "We'll wait for the lab results along with you, so that we can be sure of what it is we are looking for. Meanwhile, I think we're going to call in and get something started to isolate all the money coming in for the banks and ATMs. The sooner we can stop this tainted money getting into circulation, the sooner we might see new cases beginning to slow down."

Dione's face softened. "I'm sorry I was so harsh," she said. "This is one of the toughest situations I've ever had to deal with, and my nerves are as frayed as they have ever been. By all means, do what you can to stop it from spreading. I'm going to work on finding a way to keep some of these people from dying."

Sam and Garza thanked her and walked away. They found an empty waiting room and stepped inside, then sat down beside each other.

"Okay, how do we get the word to all the banks to stop passing out cash until it can be tested?" Sam asked.

"I don't know," Garza said. "I guess we start by calling the chief. He's going to have to talk to the mayor, and it may take the mayor talking to the governor's office. This thing is popping up in other parts of the state, so it's bigger than just here in Orlando."

He took out his phone and called Chief Olson, quickly explaining what they had concluded. The chief was shocked, but agreed to start making the necessary calls.

"What I want you to do," he said, "is talk to Prichard and see if you guys can figure out how the tainted money is getting into those banks. Whoever is doing this must have access to the money before it even gets there, right?"

"Yes, sir, and we are already on it."

The call ended and Garza turned to Sam. "Now, all we gotta do is figure out where the money comes from. If we know that, then maybe we can find out who has access to it who could do this."

"Agreed," Sam said. "And I think I know just the person to help us figure that out."

He took out his phone and hit the speed dial icon for Indie, then put the phone on speaker.

"Sam? How's it going?" she answered.

"I think we might be making some progress," Sam said. "But we need your help. I need you to put Herman to work and see if he can find out where the banks get the money they distribute. I know it comes from the Federal Reserve Branch for this part of the country, but we need to know how it is actually distributed to banks here in Florida. Put them on that as fast as you can, and then get back to me as soon as you have an answer."

"So, it really is the money?" she asked.

"It's definitely looking that way," Sam said. "Beauregard and Mom were able to confirm it for us this morning."

"I will bet your mom was happy," Indie said. "She loves to be helpful—this is probably a new adventure for her."

Sam grinned. "She does seem rather excited, yes. Let me know as soon as you have some information on that, will you? We're trying to figure out how to stop the money before it gets into circulation, but we also have to find out how the money is being treated with the chemicals that are doing this. The answer has to be somewhere in between the Federal Reserve Banks and the local banks."

"I'll get on it now, and call you back as soon as I know something."

Sam put the phone back into his pocket and looked at Garza. "Now, we wait. As soon as the doctor can confirm what we are looking for, we need to start rounding up samples of cash and have them tested."

"We can put a bunch of uniforms on that," Garza said. "The big question is still who could do this to the money. That's what we need to find out, Sam."

"One step at a time, Ed," Sam said. "One step at a time."

They returned to Doctor Dione and waited for the lab to give her confirmation of the suspected cause of the infection, and they were rewarded only a short time later. Dione read the results that were handed to her, then looked up to them with a ghost of a smile on her lips.

"You pegged it," she said. "Mir-105-C is present, along with traces of DMSO. Somehow, money is being treated with this stuff, maybe soaked in it for all I know, and then ending up where people can touch it with their fingers. The DMSO draws the Mir-105-C through the skin and into the bloodstream, and from there, it circulates and does its damage. We can treat it now, gentlemen. At least some of the victims coming in over the last hour or so will survive, and we should be able to save any new ones from here on out."

"Okay, that's great," Sam said, and Garza echoed him enthusiastically. "Now, you said this is something that comes from pancreatic cancer?"

"Yes, but not in such a concentrated form. These people are showing Mir-105-C concentrations in their blood that are at least a thousand times higher than they would be if they had that kind of cancer, which means that just touching this stuff once is enough to be fatal."

"Doctor, who would know enough about this stuff to be able to come up with this kind of poison? And where would they get so much of it?"

Dione pursed her lips in thought for a moment. "Almost anyone connected to the medical field would have heard about it," she said. "As for getting a quantity, that isn't necessarily the right way to look at it. Enzymes like this one are potent and can be diluted easily, so it wouldn't take a large quantity to accomplish what we're seeing. And accessibility wouldn't be that big a problem; any first-year chem student could make it."

Sam nodded, thinking he needed to let a couple of spooks know just how much they had accomplished. He thanked the doctor and turned to walk away with Garza following, then went directly back to where Kim was waiting.

She looked up at him curiously as he approached, noticing the odd expression on his face.

"Sam? Everything okay?"

"It's better than okay," Sam said. "Tell Mom and Beauregard that the information they got us was critical. Because of them, the doctor has figured out what the actual cause is, and she can probably come up with a treatment. Tell them they just saved a lot of lives."

Kim smiled, and a couple of tears appeared on her cheeks. "They heard you, Sam," she said softly. "They say they were glad to help."

* * *

Indie finished feeding Bo, which she had been doing when Sam called, then set him in his playpen and got out her computer. She opened it up and started entering information for Herman to search, but the chimes that indicated he had found results began before she was even finished.

"Herman? That was quick." She clicked on the first link out of curiosity and found information regarding the Federal Reserve and how it works. She scanned through it quickly and decided it was not giving her what she needed, so she moved on to the next one.

Five links down, she found what she was looking for.

Currency of the United States is made available to banks in order to make it possible for the general public to withdraw cash, whether from banks or ATMs. To move the currency from their facility to the banks, professional security companies are employed to carry it to the banks in a specific area.

She continued reading for several minutes and found out that Preemptive Security and Courier Company provided the armored cars and security guards who delivered money to banks throughout Florida. She quickly copied down the address and phone number of the main office, which happened to be right there in Orlando, and texted it to Sam, adding: *"Here's the company that hauls money for the Fed to the banks."*

* * *

Sam's phone chirped to let him know he'd received a text message, and he looked at it quickly. He read the message from Indie, then looked over at Garza, who was driving.

"Preemptive Security," he said. "That's the company that hauls money to the banks. Their HQ is on the corner of Westmoreland and Washington. Let's go have a chat with them."

"Damn right," Garza said. "See who delivers in the areas we know are affected."

He took the next left turn and they arrived at the building just a few minutes later. They parked near the front entrance and followed by Kim, who had been riding in the back seat, they made their way inside to where a receptionist looked up with a smile. Sam noticed that she was wearing a security uniform, and the pistol strapped to her hip indicated she was probably more than just the door greeter.

"Welcome to Preemptive Security," she said. "How can we help you today?"

Both men held out their IDs. "I am Detective Garza with Orlando PD, and this is Mr. Prichard. He's working with us on an investigation into the strange sickness that's been going around this area. We'd like to talk to whoever schedules your money delivery trucks."

The young woman looked the IDs over carefully, then smiled up at them again. "That would be Mr. Davidson. If you have a seat, I will call and see if he can come out and talk to you."

Sam leaned on the counter in front of her. "I don't think you understand the situation properly," he said. "It's not a matter of whether he can come out and talk to us; it's a matter of how quickly he is going to do so. We have found evidence that the sickness is a deliberate attack using certain chemicals that are being applied to money, so that when someone handles that money, they become affected. Since yours is the company that transports money into the state, we are beginning here with you. Any delay in answering our questions could be seen as obstructing an investigation into possible biological terrorism. Have I made myself clear?"

The woman, whose name tag said M. Johnson, managed to keep the smile in place, even though her eyes grew wide.

"Yes, sir," she said. "Please wait right here, and I'll get him for you." She picked up the phone and punched a button, then spoke softly but briskly as she explained why the two investigators wanted to speak with Mr. Davidson. She hung up a moment later and turned back to them, her smile barely managing to hang on. "He says he'll be out immediately, and I am supposed to direct you to the conference room. If you'll go through that door, it will be the first room on the right." She pointed to a door in the wall behind her, her face obviously pleading with them to move quickly.

TWELVE

Sam turned to Kim and suggested she have a seat in the waiting area. As she did so, Garza followed Sam to the door and through it, and then into the conference room. They had just taken chairs at the big table when Davidson stepped inside and identified himself.

"Charles Davidson," he said, holding out a hand to each of them. "Can I ask what this is all about? Millie said something about poison on the money?"

Between the two of them, Sam and Garza caught him up to speed. "Naturally, since your company handles the money when it first comes into the state of Florida, we need to begin here. Can you tell me the procedure for delivering money to the banks?"

Davidson chewed the inside of his cheek for a couple of seconds before he spoke. "Okay, that is highly secure information, but under the circumstances, I'm going to take a chance. I would like to verify your identities before I answer, though. Any objection?"

"Not at all," Sam said. He and Garza produced their IDs once again, and Davidson took a cell phone out of his pocket and dialed a number from memory.

"Chief Olson? Charles Davidson, Preemptive Security. I have a couple of men here asking questions, and I'd like to confirm that they are working with the police. Their names are..." He cut off suddenly and glanced up at the two of them again. "Yes, sir, that is them. I will give them every possible cooperation. Yes, sir, and thank you."

He ended the call and laid the phone on the table. "So, you're that Sam Prichard," he said. "Under other circumstances, I would love to pick your brain, but I don't think we have time for that today." He cleared his throat. "The procedure is pretty simple. We have two trucks that run back and forth between here and Atlanta. Every night, they pick up close to a billion dollars in new currency and bring it back here for distribution. We have a secure facility on the outskirts of Orlando where that money is separated and reloaded onto smaller trucks that deliver to the banks and other financial institutions. When they deliver, they also pick up used bills that are nearing the end of their life cycle, and those are transported back to the Federal Reserve for destruction."

"All right," Sam said. "We need to get lab technicians into that facility, to start testing the money. I don't really think we're going to find that it's already tainted, but we have to rule it out."

Davidson sucked on his cheek for a second. "Okay," he said. "What I need you to do is have your lab technicians meet us out at the guard shack there, because they won't be allowed in without my approval. How soon can we make this happen?"

Garza took out his phone and called the local crime lab, who said they had no one who could perform the tasks necessary. He ended that call while Sam called Doctor Dione at the hospital. After a brief explanation of the problem, she agreed to send two of her own CDC lab technicians, and Sam got the address from Davidson to give to her.

"Techs will be out there in about twenty minutes," he said to Davidson. "How long will it take us to get there?"

"Not more than that," Davidson replied. "Where you parked?"

"Out front," Garza replied.

Davidson, who had not even bothered to sit down during the conversation, nodded. "All right," he said. "I'll get my car and meet you out front, and you can just follow me." He turned and left the room without another word while Sam and the detective got to their feet and exited, themselves. They collected Kim on the way out, quickly filling her in on the next step in the investigation.

"You really don't expect to find anything?" Garza asked as they got into the car.

Sam shook his head. "I think that if the money was already tainted by the time it got here, we would be seeing this happening in the surrounding states, as well. I don't want to test it to look for the poisons, I want it tested to eliminate the incoming truck as the source."

"Makes sense," Garza said. "Okay, there he is." He started the car and put it in gear, then pulled in behind Davidson as he led the way out of the parking area.

* * *

"I don't know what more we can do," Grace said to Beauregard as they hovered inside the back of the car. "I mean, it's not like we're going to run into more ghosts out at this place, is it?"

"I cannot say," Beauregard replied. "Considering that our kind have a tendency to haunt places familiar to them, we could find any number of them, especially if it happens to be an older building. However, there may be other ways we can be of assistance to Samuel. After all, no one has yet invented the door that can keep us out. Suppose Samuel wants to know what is happening in an area he is not allowed to enter? We would be able to take a look and return to let him know the answer."

"Okay, I get it," she said. "Like, we are his spies, right? We can go anywhere and look at anything, no matter who wants to keep us from it."

"Indeed. And we have the added benefit that no one knows we are assisting him."

Kim cleared her throat. "You know I can hear you guys, right?" she said.

Sam looked around at her. "Are you talking to them now?"

"Yes, sorry. Beauregard wants me to tell you that they can always go to places where you can't, so if you want to know what's going on behind a locked door, they'll be more than willing to check it out for you."

Garza gave a *harrumph.* "I gotta get me a ghost," he muttered.

"Be careful what you wish for," Sam said. "They can be as much a curse as a blessing, sometimes."

They continued following Davidson out of the city and into what appeared to be a rundown industrial park. Several of the buildings were empty and in various states of disrepair, but the one at the very back of the area was clean and well-maintained.

It was also surrounded by a double row of chain-link fence that stood fifteen feet high and was topped by multiple rolls of concertina wire. Men with dogs were patrolling inside the gap between the rows of fencing, and each of them was well armed. At the guard shack near the entrance to the facility, five men holding automatic weapons were standing around a van that was marked CDC. Davidson pulled in behind the van, and Garza stopped just behind his car.

Davidson spoke to the guards, and then one of them walked back to Garza's car. "I was told that you gentlemen can enter, but the lady is going to have to wait out here. We have a break room connected to the guard shack, she'll be comfortable there and can watch some TV or something."

"All right," Sam said. He looked around at him again. "Kim, you'll have to wait here, alone. We'll be back to get you when we get finished."

"Okay, Sam," she said. "I'll wait here, all alone."

She climbed out of the car and let the guard escort her into the building. A moment later, all three vehicles were waved through the gate.

Garza cut his eyes at Sam. "That whole thing about her waiting alone," he said. "You were saying you wanted the spooks to go in with us, right?"

"That was the idea," Sam said. "Knowing Beauregard, I'm pretty sure he caught on. They won't be able to relay anything to us until we get back to Kim, but at least they can be snooping around. Never know what they might uncover."

Garza snorted again. "In a place where they sort through millions of dollars? Too bad they can't pick up a few samples and bring them out." He suddenly looked at Sam again. "You knew that was a joke, right?"

Sam chuckled. "I figured it was. On the other hand, let's not give them any ideas. I don't think they can actually touch anything, but I never really asked."

"Yeah, you guys hear that? No touchy, I was only kidding."

Davidson led them to a parking area and they got out of the cars, then introduced themselves to the lab technicians Doctor Dione had sent. There was a man and a woman, who introduced themselves as simply Tom and Janet.

"Okay," Davidson asked, "what do you guys need?"

Janet spoke up. "I figure the best bet is to simply take random samples," she said. "We need to take a lot of them, but all we have to do is put a drop of solution on each sample and see if it changes color. If it does, that means that particular bill has already been treated."

Davidson let out a sigh. "Okay, let's get at it, then." He led them all inside the building and had them sign in at another guard station before they could proceed further.

They were then led into another room that was lined with smaller rooms. Each of them was handed a white jumpsuit and a pair of slippers, then told to step into one of the dressing rooms and change. There was a locker inside where they could secure their clothing and belongings, and they were warned by a guard that they could carry nothing of their own inside. Cell phones and even their identification had to be left in the lockers.

Once they were changed, another guard escorted them into the main area of the building. Here, they saw all of the workstations where money was separated and loaded into armored trucks of various sizes. Some of them were the kind you see in movies, a heavy-duty truck with an armored body. Others looked like specially built minivans, but all of them were obviously heavily reinforced.

Davidson raised his voice. "Okay, listen up, people," he shouted. "These people," he said, pointing at Tom and Janet, "are from the CDC. They need to take random samples of the money you are working with and test them for the presence of chemicals. Stop what you are doing and step back, so they can do their jobs."

The workers seemed, for the most part, pleased at having a break, and most of them found somewhere to sit down. One or two seemed interested in the testing and tried to hover over the technicians, but Davidson told them to back off.

Janet set up on an empty workstation while Tom went from one table to another, selecting samples of currency. Most of it was wrapped in plastic, like large bricks, and he actually broke some of them open to get random samples. He carried these back to Janet, who tested each one and set it aside to wait for a result.

"How long does it take to know if you got anything?" Sam asked her.

"Only about twenty seconds," she replied. "If the compound we are looking for is present, the drops I put on the money will turn a bright red." She looked over the ones she had already done. "I'm finding nothing so far."

"I think that's all you're going to find," Sam said. "I don't really think the money is tainted by the time it comes to this location, but we had to eliminate it as a possibility. Even so, you need to be as thorough as you think necessary. We need to be able to say with relative certainty that none of the tainted money came through this facility."

"Yes, sir," she said. She accepted another stack from Tom and began testing it while he gathered up the ones she had finished and returned them to the workstations he had gotten them from.

The process went on for a little over an hour, and Sam followed the example of the workers and found a spot to sit down. There were benches scattered throughout the facility, obviously for the benefit of the employees, but there was plenty of room. He and Garza sat nearby while Janet worked.

Beauregard, on the other hand, was extremely curious about their surroundings. With Grace following, he wandered around and looked at all the workstations, then began meandering through other parts of the building.

"You expecting to find something suspicious?" Grace asked.

"Not necessarily," he replied. "However, this is an interesting place. It appears that the building itself is quite old, perhaps dating to the early part of the last century. Before my entry into the arts of war, I was an apprentice to an architect. I find the design of this building quite interesting."

They passed through a wall into another section of the building, but found that it was only a storage area. There was a lot of equipment there, some of it stacked upon other pieces, and a great deal of what most people would consider trash. Nothing of interest was found there, so they passed through another wall and into an area where several armed men were sitting around a table, playing poker.

"These must be more of the security guards," Beauregard said. "With the ones at the gate and patrolling the fence, I count more than twenty."

"Well, I'm sure they want to be prepared if somebody tries to attack the place and rob it," Grace said.

"And they do seem quite up to the challenge."

"Not that they've ever been tested," said another voice, and Beauregard and Grace turned to see a tall man dressed in an ancient-looking suit. The lapels were quite small, and he wore a bow tie around his neck.

"Oh, hello," Grace said. "I hope we didn't startle you."

The man looked at them humorously. "I don't startle very easily," he said. "However, I will admit that I don't often see others like myself around here. The last time was—oh, probably forty years ago." He walked over toward them, looking as solid as any living person, and made a bow. "Jason Reynolds, at your service."

Beauregard returned the gesture. "Henry Thomas Beauregard," he said. "I take it you have been here for some time?"

"For the most part, yes," Jason said. "I died here, back in 1939. This place was a factory, then, where we made some of the finest furniture. I was a bookkeeper, and worked in a room at the back of the building that had no exit. When the building caught fire, I was one of several who were unable to escape."

"Oh, I am so sorry," Grace said. "What a terrible way to die."

"Truthfully, I don't remember it. I would guess that I probably succumbed to the smoke and lost consciousness before death actually claimed me. I do recall watching as my charred remains were removed from the rubble, however. That was, shall we say, disturbing."

Beauregard nodded. "You said you have been here 'for the most part.' I take it you are not bound to this location?"

"I was, for quite some time. It seems that there is some hold on us for a while after we die, keeping us in a certain place or close to certain people, but I suppose it fades over time. I had tried leaving the building on numerous occasions and failed, always finding myself right back inside, but then one day I tried again and was able to walk away. I roamed around for a while, even went back to my ancestral home in Alabama, but there was nothing for me anywhere else. After being here so long, this place holds a comfort for me. I came back about fifty years ago and have remained most of the time since, other than a few wanderings about the city. I have made a few friends among our kind and visit them now and then."

"I was also tied to the place where I died for many years," Beauregard said. "But then I met a lady who could hear me speak, and from that time on, I was bound to her until just recently. This lady with me now is Grace, who only passed away a few months ago. For some reason we do not understand, she seems bound to me."

Jason looked Grace over appreciatively. "Somehow, I doubt you find her presence unpleasant," he said with a grin. "You are fortunate to have someone with you." He glanced around at the security guards, who were oblivious to their presence or conversation. "May I ask what brings you here?"

"Grace's son is an investigator, and looking into something that is happening around the city. We have been assisting him."

Jason's eyes went wide. "He can hear you?"

"Not directly, no," Beauregard said. "However, the lady I mentioned earlier who can hear me is his mother-in-law. She is waiting for us out at the guard shack, because they would not let her in."

"Really? Could she hear me? It would be nice to speak to someone who is living."

"I doubt it," Grace said. "She can hear him, but not me. If I want to tell her something, I have to relay it through Beauregard."

"A pity," Jason said. "Oh, well. Life goes on as usual, even for those of us who are dead."

THIRTEEN

The testing came to an end and Sam and his entourage thanked Davidson for his cooperation. They changed back into their own clothing, this time with security personnel watching them, and were finally cleared to leave the building. Tom and Janet said they would go back to the hospital and wait for further instructions, while Sam and Garza drove back to the guard shack to collect Kim.

She climbed into the car and Sam looked back at her. "Are they with us?" he asked.

Kim was quiet for a few seconds, then smiled and nodded. "They're here," she said. "They said it was an interesting place, but they didn't learn anything that might help you."

Sam grinned. "I didn't really think they would," he said, "not there. Tell them to stand by, though, because they might get other opportunities."

Garza's phone rang and he snatched it up and put it to his ear. "Garza," he said. He listened for a moment, then made a sound that reminded Sam of a chicken clucking. "Okay, fine," he said, sounding exasperated. "We'll be there in a few minutes."

He ended the call and put the phone into his pocket, then looked over at Sam. "TV news has demanded that the police give them some kind of information," he said. "Want to guess who's been elected?"

"You?" Sam asked with a grin.

"You don't get off that easy," Garza said. "The chief told them you were working with us, so they want to talk to you."

Sam let out a groan, but the grin stayed on his face. They arrived back at the police station a short time later and Sam told Kim to wait in the lobby while they were shown into a conference room, where several reporters were waiting. Cameras flashed and video lights struck them full force as they stepped up to the podium.

"Mr. Prichard, why are you involved in this case?" came the first question, and Sam looked at the reporter who had asked.

"I am only here as a consultant," he said. "Detective Garza is in charge of the investigation; I'm just here to throw in a few ideas when I can."

"But you've been involved in a number of national security issues," said another reporter. "Is this an actual terror attack, all these people getting so sick and dying?"

"We're not at the point of saying it is a terror attack," Sam said. "However, we can say that the victims are being targeted by someone who is behind the problem. We do not know anything about the motivation that caused this person to take these actions, so it is a little early to class it as terrorism of any kind. Next question?"

"Mr. Prichard, we've just been told that the CDC has found an effective treatment for this condition. Does that mean people will stop dying from it?"

"I'm sorry, I'm not a doctor. You'd have to speak to the doctors at the hospital about that, but I can say that I am hopeful. Enough people have died already—we need to stop that if we possibly can."

There were more questions, and Sam fielded them all the best he could. Fortunately, his experience in dealing with reporters over the past couple of years kept him on his toes, so he was not tripped up when the questions turned surprising.

"Mr. Prichard," said one reporter, "I have a confidential source who tells me that you have determined the cause of the problem is being spread through the use of money. Is that correct?"

Sam glanced at Garza, who shrugged. As far as they knew, that information had already been announced, but the reporter's question made it appear that it was still being kept quiet. Sam thought quickly and decided to go along with it.

"Yes, that is true," he said. "We are currently trying to determine just where the tainted money is coming from and how it is getting into the hands of the people who are affected. It seems to be a combination of a dangerous enzyme and another chemical that makes the enzyme pass through the skin and into the bloodstream."

"So, would you say that people need to avoid handling money?"

"I would certainly say that. We've only just arrived at that conclusion a short time ago, so I am sure the announcement was going to be made just about any moment. For the most part, I would recommend avoiding ATM machines and withdrawing money from banks, because it seems that most of the tainted money is coming from one of those sources."

There were a couple more questions, but most of the reporters were hurrying out of the room. Each of them wanted to get the information to their news editors as quickly as they could, and Sam could hear some of them composing their stories over the phone as they hurried out the door.

One reporter, a young woman, was the last one to leave, and she turned to Sam before she did so. "Any chance I can get something exclusive?" she asked with a smile.

"Okay," Sam said. "You can say that anyone who has any information about the person behind this terrible attack should call the Orlando Police Department or any other law enforcement agency and ask them to get a message to me. Is that exclusive enough?"

The woman shot him a thumbs-up sign and hurried out with her cameraman hustling behind her. No doubt she wanted to get back to their truck and beam the footage to whatever station she worked for.

"You know we may have messed up, right?" Garza asked.

"How's that?"

"I don't know if the chief was ready to let the cat out of the bag about the money just yet," Garza said. "I wonder if he was hoping we would find something, and he'd be able to use that information to confirm we had the right guy."

Sam shook his head. "Then he can get mad at me," he said. "People are dying because they don't know that the money is poisoned. I wasn't going to let that keep going on, not when they were giving me a platform to spread the word to everyone rapidly."

"Hey, I'm on your side. I'm just saying, the chief is not going to be happy you blurted that out."

"He can get happy in the same pants he got mad in," Sam said. "I'm a consultant, remember? I'm paid for my ideas, and it was my idea to get the word out as quickly as I could."

"And I agree, like I said. I ain't arguing with you, Sam."

Sam's face softened a bit. "I know, Ed," he said. "Sorry, I guess I'm just a little sensitive about withholding information that can save lives."

"Yeah, well, you ain't the only one. When they asked about the money, I was pretty surprised. I figured somebody would've already put the word out about it, you know?"

"Yeah," Sam said. "So did I." He turned toward the chief's office and heard Garza give a slight groan as he followed along.

The receptionist at the chief's office looked up and saw him, and simply motioned for him to go on in. Sam opened the door and stepped into the office, then froze. Sitting there in front of the chief's desk was none other than Harry Winslow.

"Sam, boy," Harry said. "And here I thought you were serious when you said you were going to retire."

"I did retire," Sam said. "I'm just helping out as a consultant. What brings you here, Harry?"

"Orlando isn't that far away from where I live in Bradenton. I was already planning to come over here and see what's going on before I found out you were involved. Chief Olson is an old friend, we've known each other for years. Besides, Kathy loves the shopping over here."

"Well, be sure to tell her to use credit cards, rather than cash." Sam turned and looked at the chief. "Chief Olson, I wanted to ask you why no one had announced that the greatest danger was in handling money."

Olson looked at him, and for just a second, Sam saw a glare on his face. "Mr. Prichard, I told the press office to prepare a statement to that effect a couple of hours ago. They just got it back to me as Mr. Winslow was coming in, so I hadn't had the chance to call a press conference just yet. From what I understand, however, you took it upon yourself to correct that oversight."

"You're damn right I did," Sam said. "The people need to know about this. The more people who get the word, the fewer who are going to end up at the hospital desperately trying to stay alive."

Olson's face returned to its normal calm demeanor. "Very true, and I'm glad you did that. Now, can you tell us what you may have learned since we spoke earlier?"

"Not much, I'm afraid," Sam said, "but we can rule out the new money coming from the Federal Reserve. I took a lab tech team out there where it is distributed to the banks, and they didn't find any sign that any of it had come in contact with the chemicals that cause the sickness."

"I wouldn't have suspected that," Olson said. "So, what's the next step?"

"We need to find out where the tainted money is coming from, obviously," Sam said. "I'm going to ask the CDC to bring in more people to test money at the banks, but we've also got to start looking at the ATMs. As far as we've been able to determine, most of the victims got money out of those machines, so that may be the biggest denominator yet."

Harry looked around at him. "ATMs," he said. "Might I suggest, Sam, that you bypass the ones the banks keep at their locations and look at the independent machines. Those are owned by private companies, and if ATMs are the likely source of the poisoned currency, then it would be much simpler for someone to poison the money in those."

Sam nodded. "That's a good point," he said. "I'll get Indie on it right away." He looked at the chief again. "Is there anything else we need to let the public know about?"

Chief Olson sported a glare again for just a second, but it vanished instantly. He started to speak, then picked up a piece of paper from his desk and glanced at it.

"Nothing for the public," he said, "but perhaps this is for you. A call came in just a little while ago from someone who claims to know how this outbreak got started. It was a woman, but all we have is a phone number, and when we checked it out, it turned out to be a pay phone in a local diner. I was going to send someone else, but maybe you should go and try to talk to whoever called it in."

Garza stepped forward and took the slip of paper, glancing at it before passing it on to Sam. As the chief said, it contained only a local phone number.

"We'll do that," Sam said. "Harry, great to see you. When this is over, you and Kathy better come see us at the house."

"Believe me," Harry said, "I have been hearing that from her for the last month. She wants to see the children, and I have learned how unhealthy it is to deny her anything she wants."

Sam grinned and suppressed a chuckle, and then Garza followed him out the office door. He hurried to catch up with Sam, who was moving quickly, despite his slight limp.

"You think that might be a real lead?" he asked.

"No idea," Sam said, "but we certainly can't risk passing anything up." He took his phone out of his pocket and dialed Indie.

"Hey, babe," she said. "Did the information I sent you help? I mean, it's not like you called me back to tell me."

Sam winced. "I'm sorry, honey," he said. "Yes, it did help, and that's why I didn't call back. We were so busy that it honestly just slipped my mind."

Her voice softened slightly. "Okay, I can understand that, I guess. I take it you need something else now?"

"Yes, and it is something you and Herman can do faster than anybody else," Sam replied. "I need to know about every private ATM company in the state. There are probably going to be a lot of them, so concentrate on the ones that have offices in Orlando, Miami and Jacksonville. Those are the areas where victims have been affected, so it is likely our perpetrator is working the machines in all three cities."

"Okay," she said. "I'm getting ready to feed the kids, but I will get on it right after that. Bo will be down for a nap, anyway, after he eats."

"Okay, babe," Sam said. "Let me know what you find out. I think we might actually be getting close."

"You got it. Love you, Sam."

Sam professed his love for her as well, and then ended the call. The two of them collected Kim and went to Garza's office.

"Now," Sam said. "Since the chief didn't bother to write down which diner, can you find out for us?" He handed the slip of paper back to Garza, who glanced at it once more and then passed it back.

"That's easy," he said. "That's Angie's Roadhouse. Half my snitches use that phone when they need to call me."

Sam nodded. "I suspected you might recognize it." He took out his phone again and dialed the number of the pay phone. A bored-sounding woman's voice answered on the third ring.

"Angie's," it said.

"My name is Sam Prichard," Sam said, "and I am working with the police department. Someone called from this number and said they had information about why people are getting sick."

The voice became muffled, but Sam could make out what she was saying.

"Anybody here call the cops?"

A moment later, the woman came back on the line. "Nobody here wants to admit to it," she said, but then she lowered her voice. "But I can tell you that the only person who has used the phone this morning is still sitting here. A girl, long blonde hair that looks like it hasn't been washed in a week."

"Good," Sam said. "Try to keep her there, but if she leaves, see if you can get a license number or something."

"No problemo," the woman said, and then the line went dead.

"I think we'd better head down there," Sam said. "The waitress or whoever that was says the only person who's used that phone today is still sitting there. We need to get there before she gets away."

* * *

The young woman sat quietly at her table in the diner. The old, gray tables were cracked, and there was a distinct smell of stale coffee in the air, but, other than that, it was a comfortable enough place to be when you were just waiting for someone you didn't really know.

She drummed her fingers idly on the tabletop, right beside the little pile of torn-up napkins she had made. Her nails were bitten and uneven; they were a symptom of the toll that the last few days had taken on her. There was a disheveled look about her, and the other patrons of the diner could be forgiven for thinking this was the way she normally looked. However, this couldn't have been further from the truth; most of the time, she prided herself on her appearance. She wasn't ever going to be classed as a stunning beauty, but she was a pretty girl.

Her long, blonde hair hung down to her shoulders and was cut in the latest style, but instead of being thick and full as it usually was, it hung lank and uncombed. Her blue eyes, which normally sparkled with happiness and perhaps a bit of mischief, currently appeared dull and red, as if she had been crying. Her clothes were rumpled and stained, and the rest of her seemed to fit that description as well.

It was just about noon, but she was not even hungry. She had wrestled all through the night with the decision she had finally made, and even now, she was not certain it was the right one. Still, she was not the type who could sit by and let people die.

The door opened, causing a bell to ring, and she glanced up to see two men and a woman enter the diner. One of the men was dressed somewhat casually and walked with a limp, while the other wore a suit. The woman simply seemed to be with them, not really connected to them at all. They looked around the diner for a couple of seconds and then she saw the waitress nod in her direction. Both of them turned their heads and their eyes locked onto her.

No doubt about it, she thought. *These guys are definitely cops.*

The three of them walked toward her, both of the men trying to look like they weren't paying any attention to her at all, but she was not fooled. She had no doubt they were both watching her like hawks, waiting for her to try to bolt and run. As tempting as that idea sounded, she had made her choice. It was time to go through with it.

"Hello, miss?" asked the tall one with the limp. "I think perhaps you were waiting for us?"

"Yeah, I guess," she said. "You're cops, right? Of course you are, I can spot 'em a mile away."

The two men sat down across the table from her while the woman took a seat at another table nearby. The waitress, who had been following them with a coffee pot in her hand—probably some sort of trademark of the place—flipped over a couple of cups that had been sitting on the table and poured coffee without even asking if they wanted it. She did the same for the woman at the other table, who was lingering as if she might be trying to overhear whatever conversation took place.

"My name is Sam Prichard," said the taller man, the one who was limping. "This is Detective Garza, with the Orlando Police Department. Are you the one who called and said you might know something about why people are getting sick?"

"Yeah, that was me," she said. "I'm a little sick myself, just thinking about it, to be honest."

"I think I can understand that," Sam said. "Can you tell us your name?"

"It's Emma," she said. "Emma Milligan."

Garza wrote it down on a notepad he had taken from his pocket.

"Okay, Emma," Sam said. "What is it you can tell us?"

FOURTEEN

Emma took a deep breath and then took a napkin out of the holder and began tearing it into little pieces and adding them to the pile. She glanced at the waitress, who was finally moving away.

"I think you probably know it isn't just that people are getting sick, right? I mean, you know that somebody is making them sick, right?"

Sam nodded. "Yes, we are aware of that."

She frowned, and for a second, Sam was afraid she was going to change her mind and clam up, but then she blew out a puff of air.

"Well, I know who's doing it. And I'm going to tell you, don't worry, but first I need to say a couple other things, all right?"

Sam narrowed his eyes. "Okay, Emma, we're listening."

"Sometimes, sometimes people don't get the recognition they deserve. Sometimes, for whatever reason, people who are really smart or really gifted, they get passed over and ignored while other people who aren't nearly as smart or gifted get patted on the back and told how wonderful they are. That is kinda what happened in this case. This guy, the one who's doing this, he's like this brilliant medical student. Even his instructors say he's come up with things in school that most doctors have never even thought about, and they always write about how he's destined for great things, stuff like that, you know?"

Sam nodded. Considering the way the sickness was being inflicted on people, the thought that it was the work of a medical student could make sense.

"Well, anyway," Emma went on, "this guy, he's got this problem. You see, while he's super smart and all that, he's also—well, he's pretty ugly. The poor guy had some major acne problem when he was a teenager, and he is scarred like *everywhere*. His face is really bad, little pits all over it and then he's got these big buck teeth, and—well, he sort of reminds me of Frankenstein. He is scary to look at, you know? I mean, I knew him for like six months before I could even stand to look at him. He is just scary, that's all, scary-looking, I mean. And the most ironic thing of all is that, once I got to know him, he's one of the nicest guys I've ever met in my life." She shrugged. "Or at least, he was. Anyway, to explain all this, a few months ago I made myself get over the way he looked and we got to be friends. We hung out together once in a while, and sometimes we'd, like, go to a movie together, stuff like that. It wasn't like we were dating, we were just hanging out, you know?"

She paused, and Sam sensed hesitation.

"At least, that is how you saw it, right? I get the impression he might've thought there was more to it?"

She made a face that Sam took for confirmation.

"Yeah, I guess so," she said. "And then, about a couple weeks ago, he had this really bad day when people at school were giving him all kinds of trouble. Because he looks the way he does, people pick on him a lot, you know? Well, some of the jock-type guys decided to take it up a notch and they really roughed him up. I mean, they beat him up pretty good, to be honest. Anyway, he showed up at my apartment and was all bloody and everything, so I took him in and started cleaning him up…"

"And he took your concern for something more than it was," Sam said, matter-of-factly. "Right?"

"Well, yeah," Emma said. "He—he kind of put his arms around me and tried to kiss me, and I guess I freaked out a little bit. I pushed him away and said something about it being gross, and—oh, God, the look on his face! It was just terrible, and I knew I'd really hurt his feelings, but it was too late to take it back. He got up and took off out the door, didn't even bother to put his shirt on. I tried to catch him to tell him I was sorry, but he wouldn't listen, and he just kept on running."

"Okay, Emma, I'm with you. What happened after that?"

She was quiet for a few seconds, ripping another napkin to shreds. The pile in front of her was taller than the salt shaker.

"He wasn't at school the next day, so after classes, I went to his place to look for him. He was home, but he wouldn't come to the door at first, so I kept banging on it and calling his name until he finally did. He opened it just a little bit, and I told him how sorry I was for what happened. He was real nice about it, he said he understood, he knew that he had mistaken what was going on, all that. But then he said—he said he was going to do something to show me that he was good enough for me, and I asked him what he meant. He said not to worry about it, but that I would find out in a few days. He said it was something that was going to make him famous, so maybe everybody would really start to like him. I told him he didn't have to do anything like that, that he was my friend and I was going to like him no matter what." She made another face and swallowed hard. "I even told him we could start dating, if he wanted to, but he said that would come later."

She paused again and Sam looked at her. "And you think he's the one making all these people sick? That this is something he's doing to try to become famous, so that you'll like him?"

She shook her head. "Not exactly," she said. "You see, when people started getting so sick, he called me. He told me he was going to be the one to cure all these people, to make this go away, and I asked him how he could be so sure of that. He—he laughed, Mr. Prichard. He said it helped to have a cure before the disease was even discovered."

Sam's eyes widened. "You think he was going to spread this around and let a lot of people die, then suddenly come forward with the treatment for it? That's how he wanted to become famous?"

She nodded. "Yeah, that's what he had in mind. At first, I didn't realize exactly what he was saying, but last night it kind of hit me. The only way I can see that he could have a cure before anybody discovers a disease would be if he was the one who created the disease in the first place. That means he has to be the one who is making everyone sick, right?"

"I admit it sounds that way," Sam said. "Did he tell you how he is making the people sick? What particular method he's using?"

She shook her head. "He didn't tell me that directly," she said. "I just figured it out for myself."

Sam looked at Garza. He knew they were both thinking the same thing, which was that if she was right, this medical student must have an accomplice who could get into the ATMs, or who worked with the company that handled them.

Sam turned back to Emma. "Emma, first, tell me who this is that we are talking about. Then we have some other questions for you."

She nodded sadly. "All right, yeah," she said. "His name is Danny Logan. He is a third-year medical student at UCF, and he lives in an apartment on South Downey Street. I don't know the actual address, but it's the building right across from the big Walmart. He lives in apartment twelve."

Garza wrote down the name and then walked away from the table while Sam looked at the girl, who now had tears beginning to slide down her cheeks.

"Emma, we have an idea how he is infecting people with this condition. Do you know if Danny has a job of any kind? Something connected to banks or automatic teller machines?"

She looked up suddenly. "Banks? No, he doesn't have a job at all. He got a full ride scholarship, with enough money to live on so he doesn't have to work."

Sam frowned. "Do you know if he knows anyone who has a job like that? Particularly, we are thinking of someone who puts money in ATMs. You see, the way people are getting sick is that the chemicals that cause this sickness have been embedded in money, so when people touch the money, they catch it. Most of the people seem to have gotten money out of ATMs a few hours before they got sick, so we think that is the connection."

Emma squinted her eyes as she thought, but then shook her head. "I just don't know anybody like that," she said. "And Danny, he really doesn't have any friends. I can't imagine how he could get close to money or ATMs."

Garza came back at that moment. "Sam, I got the address. It's about fifteen minutes away."

Sam looked up at him, then turned back to Emma. "Emma, we are going to go see if we can find Danny. I'd like you to stay here and wait, and we'll come back." He motioned for Kim to come closer. "This is Kim, she'll wait here with you. Okay?"

Emma took another napkin and began shredding it, but she nodded. "Okay," she said. "Just—just please don't hurt him. I think maybe this isn't all his fault, maybe it is partly my fault."

"That is nonsense," Kim said. "If this boy is the one who is doing this, then he made his own decisions. You can't take the blame for what someone else does."

Sam got to his feet. "We'll be back," he said. He motioned for Garza to lead the way, and the two of them walked out the door.

* * *

"This guy drives too slow," Grace grumbled. She and Beauregard were in the back seat of the car, riding along with Sam and Garza as they went to check out the suspect, Danny Logan.

"He seems to be doing fine to me," Beauregard replied. "You tend to be impatient, my dear."

In the front seat, completely oblivious to their invisible passengers, Sam looked over at Garza. "Think you could speed up just a bit?" he asked. "If this is our guy, I'd like to get him before he decides to take a trip to New Zealand or something."

"Impatient, ain't you?" Garza asked, but he pushed the accelerator a little further.

Grace looked at Beauregard, her face smug.

They arrived at the apartment building moments later and the two men got out of the car and hurried inside the building. Apartment twelve was on the third floor and there was no elevator, so Garza hurried up the stairs while Sam did his best to keep up. He was a floor behind by the time Garza got to the top of the stairs, but the detective stopped and waited for him.

The door to the apartment they were looking for was just a few feet down the hall. Sam knocked while Garza stood to the side, his hand on his service weapon.

There was no answer. "Mr. Logan? My name is Sam Prichard, I am working with the police. I need to speak with you."

There was still no answer. Garza raised his eyebrows at Sam.

"You should've brought the woman and the spooks," he said. "They could have gone in and told us if he's home."

Sam looked at him and rolled his eyes. "We're going to need a warrant," he said. "From what Emma said, I think we have enough information to get one."

Garza looked at the door for a moment, then glanced around the hallway. "Or we can do things the Orlando way," he said.

He walked across the hall to another door and knocked. A moment later, it was opened by a woman who kept the safety chain on as she peered out at him.

"Yeah?"

Garza held up his ID. "I am Detective Garza with Orlando PD," he said. "I'm trying to make sure your neighbor is okay. I guess his mama hasn't been able to reach him, and she wanted us to stop by and check on him. Have you seen him today?"

She looked at his ID, then pushed the door shut and took off the chain. When she opened it again, she said, "You mean Danny? I saw him yesterday for a couple of seconds, but he was talking to a couple other guys. It didn't sound like they were friends, if you know what I mean. When I came out of the stairway, they were talking kinda loud, and then they just sorta pushed him inside and shut the door as I came by. From the way it sounded, I think they were having an argument."

"Wow, really?" Garza asked. "Listen, you don't know anybody who might have the key to his place, do you? Just so we could peek in and make sure he's okay?"

"No, Danny isn't really the friendliest guy. I mean, he's always polite and everything, but that was the first time I ever saw anybody go in his apartment. Even his girlfriend never comes over here."

"Oh, he has a girlfriend? Would you know her name?"

She grinned. "It's Emma, but I don't know the last name. Sometimes when I run into him in the hall, he talks about her. She must be quite a girl; to be honest, I'm not even sure a mother could love a face like his."

Sam came closer. "Miss, you said it sounded like they were arguing. Did you get the impression Danny might've been in some kind of danger?"

"Danger? Well, I don't really know, but those guys did seem

pretty pissed off about something. They were yelling a lot, and I heard Danny say something about how he was not going to give them whatever they wanted."

Sam and Garza looked at one another. "Sounds like probable cause to me," Sam said. "We have reason to believe the occupant of the apartment could have been endangered by his recent visitors and may be incapable of answering the door."

Garza grinned. "The Orlando way," he said. "Works most of the time." He turned back to the young woman. "Thank you," he said. "You've been most helpful."

The two of them went back to Danny's apartment door and Sam tried jiggling the doorknob. It was locked, so he glanced back at the woman. She jumped when he did so and quickly shut the door, and Sam reached into his pocket. He took out a key ring and tried a couple of them in the doorknob until he found one that fit.

"Don't try this at home, kids," he said, and then he twisted the key and took out his pistol. He tapped the key several times with the butt of the gun and grinned when it suddenly turned.

Garza's eyebrows went up. "You gotta teach me that," he said. "I've only ever seen that work in movies. I thought it was just a gag."

"It works sometimes," Sam said. He turned the knob and removed his key, and they stepped inside the apartment.

FIFTEEN

The living room looked like a typical bachelor pad. There was a worn sofa with a coffee table in front of it, and a large flat-screen TV hanging on the wall. A game system sat on the coffee table with a couple of controllers, but everything was off.

"Hello?" Sam called out. "Mr. Logan?"

There was no immediate response, so they began walking through the apartment. Stepping from the living room into the combination kitchen and dining area, Garza suddenly stopped and held out a hand to indicate that Sam should pause, as well. He pointed to the floor, where a brownish stain had appeared.

"Looks like blood," he said. "Not a whole lot, but enough to mean somebody got hurt."

The stain was round and about twelve inches in diameter. Sam nodded.

"Yeah," he said. He turned to the right and stepped into a short hallway. There was an open door on the left that led to a bathroom, and he reached inside to turn on the light. The bathroom was empty, with no sign that it had been recently occupied.

Across the hall was another door. This one was closed, so Sam reached out and tried the knob. It turned easily, and he pushed the door open to look inside.

He stood there in the doorway without moving for several seconds, and Garza stepped up beside him. The detective looked over Sam's shoulder into the room and then let out a low whistle.

"Man," he said. "I've seen crime labs that didn't look that sophisticated."

The room, originally intended as a bedroom, held several tables with what Sam took to be professional lab equipment. He recognized an electron microscope with a video monitor, a centrifuge and a few other items, but there were several devices he had never seen before.

"Don't touch anything," he cautioned. "We don't know if there might be any of the active poison in there."

He turned to the left and opened the door at the end of the hallway. This one was an actual bedroom, but it looked like it had been hit by a tornado. Clothes were lying everywhere, dresser drawers lay on the floor and a lamp that had been on the nightstand was smashed against the wall. Once more, Sam only stood in the doorway and looked around, and a moment later, he turned back to Garza.

"I'm calling Dione," he said. "We need those lab techs out here. You might want to call it in as a crime scene at the same time."

"Yeah, but what's the crime? Maybe Logan is hurt, but there's no body and no sign of him."

"At the moment, I think we have enough probable cause to say he's a suspect in creating the poisoning agent. Let's go with that, for right now. We'll deal with the bloodstain after the lab techs take a look at it."

"Yeah, okay." Garza took out his phone and dialed while Sam did the same.

Police arrived first, including the local CSI team, but Sam told them all to stay out of the lab room until Tom and Janet arrived to check it out. The techs were incensed, but Garza backed him up and insisted they wait.

The CDC techs showed up about fifteen minutes later, and one look into the lab room made them climb into safety clothing and masks. They went in a few minutes later and closed the door behind themselves.

"You think we got the right place?" Garza asked.

Sam screwed up his face. "Believe it or not, I'm not a hundred percent sure. Something about this doesn't feel right. The neighbor said the men who came to see him were angry, that they were arguing. I suppose it could be the accomplices, but I'm not sure we have enough evidence to back up that assumption."

Garza shrugged. "He's got a lab, he's a medical student who knows about this kind of stuff, and he told the girl he had a cure ready. Sounds to me like he might be the brains behind it, and the other two are probably the ones who fill up the ATMs."

"That's possible, I…"

Sam's phone rang and he looked to see that it was Indie calling. "What've you got, babe?"

"Well, it turns out there are only eight companies that have private ATMs in the cities that have been affected," she said. "So, rather than just pass that information on, I had Herman do a little further digging. Did you know that every ATM machine has a security video camera pointed at it?"

"Yeah," Sam said. "I thought everybody knew that."

"Well, I did, but I wasn't sure about anybody else. Anyway, the point is, I had Herman search through all of their systems until he found access to the stored security videos. I've been going through them for the last hour, and there's one guy who has turned up at every machine owned by the company he works for. The rest of them, it is all random, but this one company seems to have only one guy servicing all their machines."

"That's excellent work," Sam said. "Can you send me a photo?"

"I can do better than that," Indie said. "I got a couple of clear shots of his face and ran them through all the facial recognition databases. He popped up in Florida's own database, so I was able to identify him. His name is Stephen Robbins, works for Orlando Monetary Services, and he lives there in Orlando. Sending you a snapshot of his driver's license right now."

Sam's phone chirped in his ear, telling him he had received an SMS message. He took the phone down and looked at the picture that appeared, then put it back to his ear.

"Fantastic," he said. "Now, I need you to do something else. See if you can find any connection between Robbins and a medical student at UCF named Danny Logan. If you find a picture of Logan, he should be easy to recognize. From what I understand, he is rather homely."

He could hear her tapping on the keyboard, and suddenly she gasped. "Homely? Sam, this guy is right past homely into seriously ugly! I know that's not a nice thing to say about someone, but holy geez!"

"Yeah, I heard all about that," Sam said. "Just see if you can find any connection between the two of them. Right now, there's a possibility Logan is the one who created the poison that is causing this epidemic, and he's also missing."

"I'm on it," Indie said, and the line went suddenly dead. Sam looked at the phone strangely for a second, then called up the picture again and showed it to Garza. "Stephen Robbins," he said. "He works for one of the ATM companies, and Indie went through their security videos. She found out that he's the only ATM service person who has turned up at machines in all the cities where the epidemic has made its presence known."

Garza looked at the photo and nodded. "Sounds like he's our man, then," he said. "Let me call it in, I can put out a BOLO for him." He took Sam's phone and held it while he dialed on his own, and Sam listened as he gave the information about Robbins to the dispatcher. Sam filled in the information about Mr. Robbins' employer, and Garza relayed that, as well. As soon as he was done, he handed Sam's phone back to him.

"Uniforms will be looking for him," he said. "They'll even go to his work and home, so if he's around, they'll find him."

"Good," Sam said. "Now, we just have to hope they find him before he can put any more of this tainted money into circulation."

* * *

"God, I hope they don't hurt him," Emma said. "I mean, I know he's doing something bad, but he really isn't a bad person on the inside."

Kim looked at her. "Sometimes good people do things that are bad," she said. "We don't always know why; sometimes even they don't know why they do them."

Beauregard, who was sitting Indian-fashion on an empty table with Grace beside him, shook his head.

"What's with you?" Grace asked. "You don't believe that good people can do stupid things?"

"Of course I do," the old soldier said. "However, I have just received one of my premonitions. This young lady's friend, Danny, is not the mastermind of this terrible crime. I am not sure of his role, but he is actually a victim, himself."

"A victim? You mean he's already died of this disease?"

"No, I don't believe that he is dead. I do sense that he is in grave danger, however." He unfolded his legs quickly and leaned toward Kim, whose eyes suddenly grew wide and round.

"Oh my goodness," she said suddenly. "I have to call Sam." She took her phone out of her purse and started to dial, then looked at the girl across the table from her. "Excuse me," she said. "I'm going to step outside for this call, so don't go anywhere."

She got up quickly and hurried to the door, then stepped out into the hot summer air. She finished dialing Sam's number and counted three rings before he answered.

"Kim? Everything okay?" Sam asked.

"I'm fine," Kim replied, "but Beauregard said to tell you that the boy, Danny, is not the one behind this madness. He is some sort of victim, himself, but Beauregard can't see anything other than that. Well, he does say Danny is in danger, but he doesn't think he's dead, yet."

"Danny is a victim?" Sam repeated. "Kim, is that all he said?"

"Yes, I'm afraid so. He said that Danny is not the one behind it, but that he is somehow a victim himself, and he's also in danger right now. That's all I've got, Sam."

"All right, it gives us something to look at. Tell Beauregard I said thank you."

Kim ended the call and softly spoke aloud Sam's gratitude, then headed back inside the diner. She had just stepped inside the door when she was roughly pushed out of the way. A man shoved by her and she saw that he was dragging Emma by one arm.

"Hey," Kim said. "She's supposed to wait here with me."

The guy looked at her for a second, as if making a decision. He reached out and snatched her phone out of her hand, throwing it hard onto the ground so that it shattered, and then grabbed hold of her own arm. "Then you can come along," he said. "I don't know what you know, but we can't have you telling anybody else."

Kim protested and tried to pull away, but his grip was too strong. Even her feeble attempts to kick at his legs did not seem to faze him as he dragged her and Emma toward a small business-type van. When they got to it, he kicked the side door once and it slid open, and Kim saw another man inside, who reached out to grab Emma. He pulled the girl inside the van while the man who had hold of her shoved Kim in behind her.

The door was slammed shut and Kim was grabbed by her hair. "Keep your mouth shut," the man who had been inside hissed at her, "and you might live to see another day." She noticed that he had a Middle Eastern accent.

Kim looked at Emma, who was shaking her head and looking frightened. The girl's eyes dropped to the floor of the van, and that's when Kim saw they were not the only unwilling passengers. A man with a face that reminded her of a bad country road was lying on the floor, apparently unconscious. He had obviously been severely beaten, because there was blood all over his face and matted in his hair.

Oh, crap, Kim thought. *That must be Danny Logan, and now Emma and I are in just as much danger as he is. Oh, Beauregard, how I wish you could use a phone to call Sam!*

Emma bent down to Danny and stroked his hair, and he moaned. A moment later, he opened his eyes and looked up at her.

"They got you," he said. "Emma, I'm so sorry. They saw you leaving my place yesterday and they beat on me until I told them who you were."

"Shh," Emma said. "It's okay. Why did they beat you up, Danny? Aren't they working with you?"

There was a sadness in his eyes as he looked at her. "No," he said. "I was actually trying to stop them, but I never got the chance." Tears began to run down his face. "I knew they were going to kill me, but now I've gotten you killed, too."

"We aren't dead yet," Kim said softly, and Danny noticed her for the first time. "Don't give up. Miracles happen."

Danny looked at the man who had been in the back with them, and who had now climbed into the passenger seat up front.

"You son of a bitch," he said. "Why couldn't you have just left her alone? She didn't know anything about you guys. You could've just left her alone."

"Yes, well, we didn't trust you. We didn't know what you might have told her, so she has to come with us now."

Danny shook his head. "If you hurt her…" he said, but he trailed off when the man picked up a spray bottle, and that's when Kim noticed that he was wearing rubber gloves. "Don't you even…"

The man squeezed the trigger on the bottle three times, spraying all three of them with what seemed like water, but Kim knew instantly what had happened.

"That's the poison, isn't it?" she asked Danny, and he nodded sadly.

"Yeah," he said. "And unless we get to a hospital soon, all three of us are going to die."

* * *

Grace and Beauregard, floating inside the van as it roared out of the parking lot, looked at one another.

"Now what do we do?" Grace asked. "Is there any way we can get word to Sam?"

"I'm afraid not," Beauregard replied. "Miss Kimberly is the only person I know who can hear me. Without her to relay our messages, I fear there is nothing we can do."

"Well, that is not acceptable," Grace said. "In the movies, when something like this happens, the ghost figures out a way to get help! It's time to be a star, Beauregard!"

The old soldier looked at her, his eyes wide and confused. "Woman, this is not a television play. We do not have the magic they use to accomplish the impossible. I have no control over who can hear me, any more than you do."

"Well, we can't just give up," Grace said exasperatedly. "We have to try something. Think, what did you do the first time to get Kim to hear you?"

"I? I did nothing. I was actually just talking to myself at the time, and I happened to notice that she seemed to have heard me. I began talking to her, but she kept shaking her head and ignoring me until the day I saw little Indie about to be hurt. I shouted at her, that day, and she finally paid enough attention to go and look for herself. Had she not, I believe the child might have been killed."

Grace shook her head. "Well, we have to think of something," she said. "What about scaring people? Do you know how to do that?"

"Scaring people? My dear, what are you talking about?"

"Oh, come on, you've been around Kim long enough to know that ghosts are supposed to be scary. How do we scare people?"

Beauregard rolled his eyes. "I would have no idea," he said. "If you knew how difficult it is to even make our presence known to the living…" He suddenly turned to look at her again. "Perhaps," he said slowly, "perhaps there is a way."

"Okay, how?" Grace asked.

"Let me think for a moment," he said. Grace managed to sit quietly for a couple of minutes while he did so, and then he turned to her again.

"I think I have it," he said. "As you pointed out, we simply need to frighten these two men."

Grace broke into a smile. "Okay, now you're talking fun! How do we do that?"

The smile that Beauregard matched her with had a hint of wickedness in it.

SIXTEEN

Sam put the phone back into his pocket and turned to Garza, motioning to the detective to follow him away from the others in the apartment.

"That was Kim," he said quietly. "Beauregard just told her that Danny is not the man we're after, that he's somehow a victim of this thing, and he's in danger right now."

"Wow," Garza said. "Did he say…"

"That's all he got. He gets flashes, but not a lot of details. We need to figure out how Danny fits into this, and it sounds like we need to do it fast."

Garza nodded. "Gotcha," he said. "Any idea where we start?"

"Not yet," Sam replied. "And if you come up with an idea, let me know quick. That damn ghost never seems to be wrong, so we need to save this kid if we can."

* * *

Herman chimed again, and Indie clicked the link that appeared on the screen. It was a link to a social media profile for Danny Logan on a website called elifecentral.com, and it showed that Stephen Robbins was on his friends list, which only had about a half dozen names. Herman had hacked into Danny's account, which enabled Indie to see his messages. She clicked on Robbins' name in the message box.

There were a number of messages, dating back almost a month. The most recent ones came up instantly, and her eyes went wide when she read them.

"Don't even think about trying to interfere with us now," Robbins had said. "One phone call to the police and you take the fall for all of this."

Danny had replied, "All I did was write a paper for you, you can't blame me because you used it to murder a bunch of people. I am trying to save them, you idiot. Remember that I can make that phone call just as easily as you can."

Indie clicked back and went to the earliest message between the two of them.

"Hey, Danny, this is Steve Robbins. I know you don't know me, but my sister is in your class and she said you could help me out with a problem. I'd be willing to pay for your help."

"Sure, man," Danny had replied. "What do you need?"

"I am a couple years ahead of you, and I'm supposed to write a term paper for my class on bioterrorism and its effects on medicine. We're supposed to come up with a new kind of bioterror attack, something that could be used to create confusion in a society. Any ideas?"

A couple of minutes passed before Danny replied again. "I can think of a couple possibilities," he said. "If you really want to blow your instructor's mind, it should be something so simple that it is easy to do, but difficult to define the symptoms. That would make it hard for anyone to work out an effective treatment, so it would be highly effective as a terroristic threat."

"And you think you could come up with something like that?" Robbins asked. "That sounds pretty awesome."

"Sure, that would be easy. You want to use some commonly

available drug that has the potential for a devastating side effect, then work out a vector to infect as many people as possible over a short period of time. If it was totally or almost totally fatal, the effect would be demoralizing on any society. That's the goal of terrorism, right? To break down the confidence of the people in the government's ability to protect them."

"Yeah, that would be perfect! Of course, we are supposed to go into detail about how the infecting agent would be made and how it would be vectored into the population. Are you really good enough to do that? It would have to be completely accurate, so the instructors can tell it could really be done. That is one of the requisites of the assignment."

"I can do it," Danny had said. "The question is, how much are you willing to pay?"

"How would a hundred dollars sound?"

"Like a joke. I'm thinking more like a thousand. We're talking about a lot of research, here, plus the time to write it up."

Robbins did not reply until a couple of hours later.

"I can't do a thousand," he said. "Would you settle for five hundred? I can scrape that together."

Another hour passed before Danny answered him.

"Tell you what. You give me the five hundred and I will write the paper for you this time, but this is a one-shot deal. I will guarantee you'll get a good grade on it, but the next time you need my help, the price goes up."

Robbins answered instantly. "You've got a deal. I can send you the money through the student credit union, will that work?"

"Sure. You got my email address? That is all you need to send it to me."

"Yeah, I've got it. I will send the money right now. How soon can you have the paper done?"

"Give me a couple days. Like I said, it's a lot of research."

There was a gap of several minutes, and then Danny messaged again. "Okay, got the money. I will have this ready for you by day after tomorrow."

The next message was from Danny to Robbins, dated two days later.

"I got it done. Sending it as an attachment." The message had an attached document, and Indie downloaded it. It opened on her monitor and she tried to read it, but the terminology was beyond her comprehension. She skimmed through it to the bottom, where a paragraph described the likely effects of the chemical agents involved.

"The introduction of concentrated Mir-105-C, which is easily synthesized in the laboratory, directly into the bloodstream will cause a breakdown of the endothelial cellular matrix. A solution of Mir-105-C in a fifty percent dilution of dimethyl sulfoxide, placed on surfaces that will be touched by the fingers, will suffice to deliver an effective dosage. This will effectively destroy the endothelial layer in all blood vessels throughout the body within a period of two to three hours, allowing blood cells to pass unimpeded through the arterial and venal walls. The effect will cause a rapid and sudden drop in blood pressure, resulting in sudden disorientation followed quickly by loss of consciousness. A secondary symptom will be exsanguination through every possible exit point of the body, including the eyes, ears, nose, mouth, urethra and rectum, leading to death within twenty-four to thirty-six hours, depending on attempts to combat the blood loss. The emotional effect upon witnesses would be immensely satisfying to any terrorist."

Her eyes wide, Indie read the paragraph again. By the time she completed it the second time, she was almost gasping for breath.

There was no response from Robbins until several hours later.

"This is incredible," he had said. "Would there even be a way to treat this?"

Danny must have been sitting at the computer, because he answered only a few seconds later.

"You didn't ask for a treatment," he had typed. "You just wanted the attack itself. If you want a treatment for it, that will cost extra."

"No, that's okay. I just wondered if it would even be possible to come up with a treatment."

"Of course it would. There are a few drugs that would interfere with the effect, even stop it completely. If people were treated quickly, they could be saved."

"Okay, I just wondered. Would it be easy for a doctor to figure out?"

"Not likely. Mir-105-C doesn't show up on any of the normal tests doctors would do while trying to identify the cause of these particular symptoms. They would have to know what they were looking for, and there are very few doctors who would even think of its side effects in this context."

"Sounds like exactly what I need, then. Thanks for the great work."

There were no more messages for quite some time, the next one coming three days earlier, the same day Garza first came to see Sam.

"I've been watching the news," Danny said in a message to Robbins. "Something sounded familiar, so I started doing a little checking. There is no Stephen Robbins listed as a student at UCF Medical School. I don't know who you really are, but you took my work and put it into real use. What the hell is your game?"

Robbins came back almost immediately. "It's not a game," he had typed. "It's called equalization! People need to learn that wealth and privilege are not all they are cracked up to be! People think money is everything, so I am using the very money they love so much to show them just how vulnerable and weak they really are!"

There was a gap of almost a minute before Danny responded.

"What on earth are you talking about? Money?"

"That is the beauty of this thing," Robbins replied. "You came up with the idea of mixing this stuff with DMSO and putting it on things people would touch. Well, I found something everybody touches. Money. That is the thing that drives everybody, and now it is the thing that is going to kill a lot of them. All I have to do is spray it on the money and put it in the ATM. They are killing themselves, and they don't even know it."

"You're absolutely insane, do you know that? Do you honestly think I am going to stand by and let you get away with this?"

"Do you think you have a choice? Remember, you are the one who figured out how to create this event. Do you want the world to know that?"

There was no response from Danny at that time. The next message he sent was the following day, Sam's first day of working in Orlando with Garza.

"I'm going to stop you," he had said. "Remember you asked me whether doctors could find a treatment? Well, they haven't, but I have, and I'm taking it to them."

That brought her back to where she had begun.

"Don't even think about trying to interfere with us now," Robbins had said. "One phone call to the police and you take the fall for all of this."

Danny's response came only seconds later. "All I did was write a paper for you, you can't blame me because you used it to murder a bunch of people. I'm trying to save them, you idiot. Remember that I can make that phone call just as easily as you can."

That was the end of the conversation, but a quick look at the timestamps told Indie that Danny had remained on the website for another twenty minutes. There was no activity on the site, so he must've been doing something else for that time, but then he logged off, or was logged off automatically for inactivity.

She quickly copied the messages into an email and sent it to Sam, then called him. "Sam," she said when he answered, "I just sent you an email. Danny Logan was tricked into writing up how to make the stuff that is doing this, but he's not actually involved. The other guy, Robbins, he's the one doing this!"

"Beauregard had your mom call and tell me that Danny is innocent, that he's actually some kind of victim, so that makes sense. Did you find any information on where we might find either of them? Danny is missing, and we just heard that Mr. Robbins is making himself scarce."

"I haven't found anything like that," Indie said. "I found this, and thought it was important enough to get it to you right away. I will see what I can find on Stephen Robbins now. Maybe there will be something that will tell me where he might go if he was hiding."

"Good girl," Sam said. "Let me know."

* * *

"I haven't done this for a long time," Beauregard said. "It was something I once occupied myself with, a sort of recreational activity, I suppose."

"Beauregard, honey," Grace said, "will you just cut to the point?"

Beauregard allowed himself a slight smile; he often wished Grace would do the same thing, stop talking and get to the point she was trying to make.

"It's the only way I know to make someone other than Miss Kimberly aware of us. I suppose you might call it a form of possession. What I do is step into a person and—I suppose that I force my will onto them. It takes a great deal of energy and I can only do it for a few moments at a time, but it's the only thing I can think of."

Grace's eyes lit up. "We can do that?"

"Yes, but as I said, it takes a great deal of energy. When I do this, you will probably not see me again for a while. I will be depleted, not even able to manifest myself to you." He pointed at Kim. "I will be back in our place in her mind, so you can find me there if you need me. I think it would be best, however, if you remain outside and watch what is happening."

She nodded. "Okay," she said. "I will only come in to you if I need you to relay something to Kim."

Beauregard shook his head. "It wouldn't matter," he said. "I will not even have the energy to communicate with her. Just watch, and I should be recovered within an hour or so." He looked at the swarthy man who was sitting in the passenger seat, looking back at the captives, and started to move toward him.

"Hold on, Beauregard," Grace said. "If something happens, you are the only one who can tell Kim what to do. Maybe I should be the one to try possessing one of these guys. How do I do it?"

Beauregard looked at her, and for a moment, he thought about telling her she was being silly, but then the logic of her statement became clear to him. If she could orchestrate something that would allow Kim and the others to escape, it would be up to Beauregard to let Kim know what to do.

"As much as it pains me to say it, you're making sense." He seemed to sigh. "What you must do is force yourself into his body, and then make yourself feel it. For a short time, once you reach that point, you will be able to exert your will over his. You will be able to move his hands and arms, to speak, and he will only be able to watch in horror. This is why I said it was recreational, because I used it on people who were rude or annoying."

Grace's eyes were big and round. "I can think of a few people like that," she said. "And at the moment, it's these two bastards. What should I do?"

Beauregard looked at the two men for a moment, then turned back to her. "You know how to drive one of these vehicles," he said. "Perhaps you could go to the driver and force the vehicle to stop in some way that would allow these ladies to escape."

Grace looked at the driver, then looked down at Kim, who was still sitting on the floor beside Emma and Danny. A wicked grin of her own spread across her face.

"That gives me a good idea," she said. "Tell Kim that they need to brace themselves. I will make it stop, all right. You just tell them to be ready to run as soon as it does."

Beauregard looked at her for another couple of seconds, then leaned toward Kim and vanished. Grace waited until Kim's eyes opened wide, signifying that Beauregard was talking to her, and then made her move.

SEVENTEEN

Tom and Janet opened the door and came out of the room. Both of them had taken off the masks they were wearing to prevent breathing in any infectious microorganisms.

"It's all clean," Tom said. "There is no sign of the enzyme anywhere in the lab. Matter of fact, what we found was a lot of notes on the use of platinum agents to combat the infection."

Sam nodded. "I just received some other information that indicates this young man was actually trying to stop the people behind the attack," he said. "He had just told them that he had found a cure for it and was planning to provide it to the doctors who were treating the patients. At the moment, we suspect they may have come after him, and that he is personally in danger."

"From what I saw," Janet said, "you're on the right track. This guy was working out a way to keep people from dying, and it's pretty ingenious. The platinum molecule actually absorbs this enzyme, neutralizing it, while at the same time acting as a catalyst for the repair of the endothelial cells. His work is probably better than what Doctor Dione is using right now. With your permission, I'd like to make a copy of his work and send it to her."

"Do it," Sam said. "If it helps even a little bit, it's worth it."

"Yeah," Garza said. "And if we don't manage to save the guy, at least his death won't be completely in vain. He is a hero, in my book."

"I agree," Sam said, "but I have no intention of letting him die if we can stop it. Let's get out of here. The uniforms can handle this place, but we need to work on finding Stephen Robbins."

Garza waved a hand to indicate that Sam should lead the way, and they headed out to the car. As they got inside, he looked over at Sam.

"Where are we headed, Chief?"

"Orlando Monetary Services," Sam said, and rattled off the address he had already looked up. "That's where Robbins works, so maybe someone there will have an idea where we can find him."

* * *

Officers Davidson and Phillips had been having a quiet day. They had made a couple of simple traffic stops, issued tickets, and spent the rest of the morning simply patrolling their part of the city. The traffic seemed lighter than usual, and Phillips, sitting on the passenger side, commented on it.

"It's because of all these people dropping dead," Davidson said. "Makes a lot of people afraid to leave home. Lotta people stay home, there's not as much traffic on the streets."

"I guess that makes sense," Phillips replied. "Makes our job easier, right?" He chuckled.

"Thank God for small favors," Davidson said. "You ready for a break?"

"Anytime. I could use a cup of coffee about now."

Davidson pulled the car into the parking lot of a convenience store, then took some money out of his pocket and passed it to Phillips.

"Bring me a large coffee, and maybe some of those little crunchy doughnuts," he said. "Get what you want, too. I'm buying today."

"Thanks," Phillips said as he got out of the car. He walked into the store and Davidson leaned back in the seat as he waited. He had just closed his eyes for a second when the radio squawked.

"All units, we just had a report of two women apparently abducted by a man from Angie's Diner on Atlanta Avenue. Witnesses say a large man with red hair dragged one woman out of the diner and then grabbed another one outside, forcing them into a vehicle and driving away. Vehicle is described as a small commercial van, red in color. No markings, no license number."

Davidson sat up and looked around, but there were no commercial vans in the immediate area. He figured somebody else might respond, and Atlanta Avenue was some distance away, anyhow. He started to lean back again as Phillips came out the door of the store.

Phillips climbed into the car and passed over the coffee and doughnuts, then buckled his seat belt.

"Okay, I'm ready," he said.

Davidson put the car in gear and pulled out of the parking space, then swung around to exit onto the street. He had just put on his turn signal when a small, red van drove across the intersection to his right.

"That look like a commercial van to you?" he asked.

Phillips looked around. "Sorry, I didn't see it in time. Why?"

"Report came over the radio," Davidson said. "Somebody grabbed a couple women from a diner on Atlanta and stuffed them into a little red van." He turned to the right and then made another turn at the intersection, just in time to see the red vehicle he had spotted make a left turn about a block ahead.

"I think we're going to check that out," he said. He pressed the accelerator and hurried toward the next intersection, then flashed his lights as he made a quick left turn. The little red van was about half a block ahead, so he pushed the car to get up behind it quickly.

He was about to turn on his lights when the van suddenly sped up and veered to the left. He watched in surprise as it jumped the curb on the opposite side of the street and drove headlong into a stand of small trees.

"What the hell?" he asked rhetorically, then turned on his lights and quickly pulled over to that side of the street. He stopped beside the curb and got out of the car.

* * *

Grace slid into the body of the driver and positioned her ethereal body so that it matched his. She tried to fold her fingers into his own and turn the wheel, but nothing happened. She tried again, feeling some kind of strange exertion go through herself, and suddenly felt as though she somehow snapped into place.

"Oh, yeah," she said, and was startled when the words came out of the mouth of the driver.

His passenger looked over at him. "What?"

Grace turned her/his head and looked at the guy, then turned back to the road. "Nothing," she said aloud, and then shoved her foot to the floor and whipped the wheel to the left. There was a small park or something over there, and she saw what looked like a thick bunch of bushes or small trees, and aimed straight for it.

"What are you doing?" said the passenger. "Are you crazy?"

"Damn right!" Grace said. The van hit the curb and bounced upward, then crashed down hard and she held tight to the steering wheel as it plowed into the brush. There was water behind it, and the front end of the vehicle splashed down into it. It came to a sudden stop, and the engine made a loud rattling noise as it died. The passenger's face had slammed into the dashboard, leaving him stunned, while the driver had crashed into the steering wheel with his chest.

Suddenly, Grace felt like she was out of breath and about to pass out. She lost her grip on the driver and sensed herself falling away, and then she was sitting on one of the imaginary chairs in the cabin she shared with Beauregard. She was exhausted, and felt as though she couldn't even move.

"Beauregard," she whispered. "It's all up to you, now."

* * *

The driver and passenger were trying to shake off the crash, but they weren't looking into the back of the van. Kim, Emma and Danny had braced themselves, just as Beauregard had told them to do, so they weren't as stunned as the other two men. Kim reached up and grabbed the handle of the side door and pulled, and it popped open easily. She hopped out and waited as Emma and Danny followed, and then the three of them took off running back toward the street.

A police car pulled up to the curb and an officer climbed out of it. Kim thought it was one of the most beautiful things she had ever seen, but then a voice screamed behind her and a gunshot rang out. The policeman stopped, looked down at himself and then collapsed to the ground, and all three of them stopped running.

Another officer came out of the passenger side of the squad car, his weapon drawn and in his hand. "Freeze!" he shouted, and Kim raised her hands, praying that the other two would do likewise. Behind her, she heard the men cursing, and then splashing as they ran away through the water.

"Officer, we were kidnapped," Kim shouted. "We were just trying to escape!"

"Get on the ground," Phillips shouted at them, and they all three quickly obeyed. Phillips came out from behind the car and hurried over to his partner. "Davidson? Davidson, are you okay?"

Officer Davidson looked up at him, his breath ragged. "Took it on the vest," he said hoarsely. "Knocked the wind out of me, but I'll be okay."

Phillips kept his weapon trained on the three who were lying on the ground while he helped Davidson sit up. When he was mostly vertical, Davidson reached out and put a hand on Phillips' gun, pushing it downward.

"They didn't do it," he said. "It was the guy behind them, but he took off. I think maybe those are the women who got kidnapped."

Phillips nodded. "That's what they were yelling," he said. "I just wasn't sure what was happening, so I told them to get down. You sure you're okay?"

"Other than some bruised ribs," Davidson said. "Help me get up, will you?"

Working together, they got him back on his feet a moment later and the two of them walked over to the escaped captives. "Come on, folks," Davidson said, "you can get up now." He held out a hand, but Danny pulled both girls back. Davidson looked at him strangely, then lowered his hand again. "I was just trying to help," he said. "What was all that about?"

"I'm afraid it's about me," Danny said. "It's a long story, but right now the three of us need to get to a hospital. We've been infected with the thing that is killing people, and it's still wet. That's why I didn't want you to touch us, so you didn't get it on you. Please, call an ambulance. They'll know how to take precautions while they get us to the hospital."

Davidson and Phillips looked at one another, and then Davidson took out his phone. He called for an ambulance to their location, and then he and Phillips stood a few feet away from the three victims to wait for its arrival.

"Beauregard?" Kim whispered while no one was looking. "Are you here?"

"I am," she heard. "You did very well, Miss Kimberly. Very well, indeed."

"Couldn't have done it without you and Grace. Is she all right?"

"She is resting. What she did took all her energy, and it will be some time before she recovers, but she will be fine." He chuckled. "For somebody who's dead, anyway. I have something I must do. I think you are in the best possible hands right now, so I will find you when I am finished."

"Okay," Kim whispered as an ambulance pulled up behind the squad car.

Danny explained what happened to the paramedics, and the medics also stayed back while the three of them climbed into the back of the ambulance. The paramedics rode up front as they headed toward the hospital.

Kim looked at one of the paramedics. "Could you make a phone call for me, please?" she asked. "I'm afraid my phone got broken."

* * *

Sam's phone rang and he glanced at it, but didn't recognize the number. It was an Orlando number, however, so he answered it.

"Prichard," he said.

"Mr. Prichard? This is Dale Simmons, I am a paramedic with the city. I have a woman in my ambulance who says she needs you to meet her at the hospital. Her name is Kim Perkins."

Sam's eyes popped open wide. "Kim? Is she hurt?"

"She's not injured, Mr. Prichard, but she says that she and two others have been infected with the cause of the bleeding sickness. She had been abducted, along with two other people, and managed to escape with the help of a couple of police officers."

"What hospital are you taking them to?" Sam asked. "Can you go to Orlando Regional?"

"That's where we're headed," Simmons said. "We should be there in about seven minutes."

"All right, tell her that we'll meet her there." He ended the call and put the phone back in his pocket, then turned to Garza. "We need to get back to the hospital," he said. "Kim is on the way there—she and a couple other people have been infected. They said something about her being kidnapped, so it's possible she actually came face-to-face with Mr. Robbins."

Garza didn't bother to ask any questions, but simply turned at the next corner and put the lights on as he headed toward the hospital. It took them almost fifteen minutes to get there through the city traffic, and the two of them rushed inside as soon as the car was parked.

Sam found Kim in the ER, tucked into one of the examination rooms. She was sitting up on a gurney, dressed in a hospital gown.

"Hi, Sam," she said with a smile. "You can relax, I'm fine."

"Fine? I heard you were infected with this stuff. What the heck is going on?"

"Oh, I was infected," she said. "That jerk sprayed it right on me and Emma and Danny, but the doctors say we're going to be just fine. It hadn't even had time to really get started on us yet, so they were able to start us on treatment that will stop it from doing any damage." She held up her arm so he could see the IV line attached to it, and her smile got a little wider. "Would you believe Danny was the one who came up with the best treatment?"

"Danny Logan? Yeah, I sort of found that out. How did you end up with him?"

"Well, it turns out that the bad guys had kidnapped him and they made him tell them about Emma, because they saw her leaving his apartment. I don't how they tracked her down to the diner, but they did, and they were trying to drag her off when I said she was supposed to stay with me, so they took me along with them."

Sam stared at her for a couple of seconds. "They said you escaped. How did you manage to escape?"

"Well, that was actually your mom's doing," Kim said. "She possessed the guy who was driving and made him crash the van, but Beauregard warned us—well, he warned me and I warned them—that something was going to happen, so then we jumped out and started running. There was a cop who saw the crash and stopped to see what was happening, and they tried to shoot him, but he was wearing a bulletproof vest. His partner jumped out of the car and the bad guys ran away, and then they called an ambulance to bring us to the hospital." She glanced around to make sure no one else was listening, then whispered, "Sam, Beauregard isn't here. I think he went after the bad guys."

Sam blinked and shook his head. "I'm sure that's all going to make sense later," he said. "But you are okay? Where's the doctor? I want to talk to him."

"Mr. Prichard, I am not a him," Doctor Dione said, coming into the room behind him. "And yes, she is going to be fine. They were sprayed with the raw form of the mixture, but they got to us quickly enough that we can stop any serious damage before it occurs. Incidentally, that Logan boy is brilliant. His breakdown of how to treat this condition is far better than what I had come up with."

Garza, who had waited outside while Sam spoke to his mother-in-law, poked his head into the room. "Everything's okay?" he asked.

"Looks like it," Sam said. "Now, as for Danny Logan, where is he? We need to talk to him."

"Two rooms down, on the left," Dione said. "He looks a lot worse off than he is, but he took a serious beating. As for the infection, he's also going to be fine."

Sam looked back at Kim. "You just sit tight and I'll be back," he said. He motioned for Garza to follow and went in search of Danny Logan.

EIGHTEEN

"I don't know what you were thinking," the swarthy man said. "Why did you crash the car?"

"I don't have any idea," Robbins answered. "I don't even know what happened, it's like I fell asleep or something. I mean, I wasn't asleep, I just—I saw my hands turn the wheel, I felt my foot hit the gas pedal, I even heard myself talking to you, but I have no idea what I was doing. It was—it was like I was possessed, or something."

"You're crazy, that's what you are. Now the police are going to know all about us."

"Well, what does it matter? We already got a lot of people, so maybe we made the point."

The other man shook his head. "Crazy," he said again.

The two of them were crouching in an alley, hiding behind a dumpster. They had made it out of the park into a small commercial area, and Robbins figured that when Hussein had shot the policeman, it had given them the distraction they needed to get away. There were undoubtedly patrol cars cruising the area, looking for them, but they hadn't seen one yet.

"Well, what do we do now?" he asked. "I guess it's time for us to get out of the country, right?"

Hussein looked at him. "Out of the country? You're insane, you really are. Now that you've been identified, they'll never let you onto an airplane. No, we must continue with our mission. We still have the formula, and I have the one bottle. That's enough for many more victims. We only need to go to different cities, now, because the ones we've already chosen will know how to cure the sickness."

Robbins looked at him for a moment. "Why bother? We were supposed to let people know that money was the real danger to them, right? I think we made the point. The cops know it was the money now, so that's all over the news. People are going to be scared of money for a long time to come."

"You and your cause," Hussein said. "Do you really think we care about making your people afraid of money? It's not about the money; it's about showing your people that they are not safe. They need to know that your government can't protect them, and that is the real nature of our mission."

Robbins cocked his head to one side and looked at Hussein for several seconds longer, then shrugged his shoulders. "Whatever, man," he said. "Long as I get paid, I don't care. Where you want to go next?"

"We need to get out of this city, first. For that, we need a car. Go and steal one, and then pick me up."

"Steal a car? Man, that's not exactly in my wheelhouse."

Hussein shook his head. He had asked himself several times why Allah had led him to this idiot. Ever since he had been dropped on the Florida coastline, the advance man for the latest jihad against the Americans, he had prayed diligently for someone to help him accomplish his mission, but all he got was Robbins.

"Then we shall steal a car together," Hussein said. "Come along, and leave your gun behind. Guns will only attract unwanted attention, and all we need is a car. Come, come, I will show you how it's done."

He got to his feet and started out of the alley, and Robbins got up to follow. There were a number of stores in the surrounding area, and Hussein started toward one that seemed only about half full. Cars were entering every minute or so, and leaving just about as often.

They walked toward the store in the center of the lot and Robbins noticed that his partner was watching all the traffic coming in and out. Hussein spotted a woman carrying a bag as she moved toward a car at the far end of the lot, and turned to follow her.

"Excuse me, ma'am," Hussein said, his accent vanishing suddenly. The woman stopped and looked around, giving him a smile.

"Yes? Can I help you?"

He smiled until he got close to her, then reached out and grabbed hold of her arm. "Your car keys," he said gruffly. "Give them to me now." His accent was back.

The woman looked frightened, and she quickly handed over the keys that she already had in her hand. Hussein let her go and started toward the car she had obviously been approaching, pressing a button on the key fob to unlock it.

As soon as his back was turned, the woman shoved her hand down in her purse and came out with a small revolver. She pointed it at Hussein and yelled, "Hey!"

Hussein ignored her and kept moving toward the car, but Robbins saw what was happening. He broke into a run and grabbed hold of the woman, yanking her arm to the side. She slapped at him with her other hand, forcing him to let go for a second, and then pointed the gun at him and pulled the trigger.

Hussein heard the shot and spun around just in time to see Robbins fall to the pavement. He sprinted back toward the woman, who was staring at the man she had just shot, struck her once in the face and yanked the pistol away. He looked down at Robbins and saw him gasping for breath. The bullet had struck him just left of center mass, puncturing his right lung. There was no way he was going to be able to get up and walk, so Hussein shook his head once and then raised the pistol and fired a shot into his head.

The woman began screaming at that point, so he turned away from her and hurried to the car. He got in and started it up, slammed it into reverse and backed out of the parking spot, then yanked it into drive and raced onto the street. He could hear people shouting as he did so, but he had wheels and was not about to stop for anyone.

Beauregard had been watching them as they waited in the alley, having followed them from the park. He was hoping to find out where they were going to hide, so he could return to Kim and get the information to Sam, but this series of developments had thrown him off. He had slipped into the car with Hussein, an unseen passenger riding shotgun as the terrorist tried to make his way out of the city.

* * *

Danny looked up as Sam and Garza entered the room. Sam was actually taken aback by his appearance at first, because the description Emma had given simply did not do the young man justice. Sam had seen ugly people before in his life, but this man could win best costume at any Halloween party without even bothering to try.

"You the cops?" Danny asked. "Mrs. Perkins said some cops are gonna want to talk to me."

"He's a policeman," Sam said, pointing to Garza. "Detective Garza with Orlando PD. My name is Sam Prichard. I'm working with him on the investigation into the bleeding sickness."

Danny nodded. "Yes, sir," he said. "I'll be happy to help in any way I can."

Sam smiled at him. "I appreciate that, Danny," he said. "What can you tell me about the men who abducted you?"

"Well, the one guy is Steve Robbins," Danny said. "He contacted me a few weeks ago and said he was a medical student who needed help with an assignment. He claimed he had a sister in my class who told them I was the guy to come to, so when he offered to pay me to help, I agreed. He wanted me to write something up for a class on bioterrorism. He said he was supposed to come up with a theoretical bioterror agent and method of vectoring, so I thought about it a little while and wrote something up for him. It wasn't until a few weeks later when I saw the news stories about the so-called bleeding sickness that I knew he had put my formula to work. I got hold of him and asked what he thought he was doing, and he threatened to turn in the paper and let me take the blame. I figured the only hope I had was to get to the doctors and show them how to cure the sickness." He shrugged. "I figured, maybe then people might believe me when I said I wasn't the one who was doing it."

"Believe it or not," Sam said, "we've already figured a lot of this out. The CDC lab techs who checked out your lab in your apartment found your notes on the cure, and they said it was brilliant. The doctor says your work is making it possible for her to save many more lives." He grinned. "I suspect there might be a job offer waiting for you when you get out of school."

Danny grinned sheepishly, but it almost looked like a grimace on his face. "Anyway, that was Steve. The other guy, he said his name was Hussein. He's from the Middle East, somewhere, but I don't know where." He raised his eyebrows. "I can tell you this, though," he said. "Hussein didn't give a rip about Steve and his phony agenda. He was here to do a lot more damage."

"What you mean by that?" Garza asked.

Danny turned to face him. "Steve had some cockamamie story

about how people with money are the big problem in our country, and how he was trying to make it so everybody would be afraid of money. I'm not sure how he was doing it, but he had some way to get the agent onto money in ATM machines. That way, whenever people got money out of the machine and touched it, they got infected. Hussein, though, he did not care a bit about Steve and his stupid ideas. Whenever Steve was out of earshot, he would ask me lots of questions about other ways to use the agent." He pointed at his own face. "The bruises are because I tried not to answer, but—to be honest, I couldn't take that much beating." His face took on a look of pure shame. "I told him what he wanted to know, even to the point of giving up the only girl who ever treated me like a person."

"I met Emma," Sam said. "She seems like quite a girl."

Part of the smile returned to Danny's face. "She's the best," he said. "I just wish—well, I wish I hadn't told them who she was."

Sam nodded. "I understand," he said. "Listen, Danny, tell me more about Hussein. Did he ever talk about anyone else helping him?"

"I didn't really know him," Danny said. "I never even met him before they dragged me out of my place. The only one I ever saw with him was Steve, but I know he made some phone calls." He squinted. "Now that I think about it, he only made phone calls when Steve was away, too. I couldn't understand anything he said, he was speaking Arabic or something."

Sam looked at him for a couple of seconds, then took out his phone. "Danny, I want you to think real hard. When he dialed, did it seem like he was dialing a regular number, or did it seem longer than usual?"

Danny's eyes rolled up toward the ceiling as he thought about it, then he looked back at Sam. "Definitely longer," he said. "Like an overseas call, I think."

Sam nodded. "Okay, can you think of anything else we need to know about them?"

Beside Sam, Garza's phone suddenly went off. He turned and walked away while he answered, but then stopped and called out to Sam.

"Sam? That guy Robbins? Somebody just blew him away in the Shop-A-Day parking lot."

Sam looked at Garza for a moment, then turned back to Danny. "Did they have guns?"

"They definitely had them," Danny said. "Trust me, I looked down the barrel a couple of times, and they shot that police officer who stopped to try to help us."

Garza was listening to the phone, and a moment later, he put it away and returned to Sam. "The gun belonged to a woman—she had a concealed carry permit. Two guys tried to take her car, so she pulled out the gun and one of them attacked her. She shot him, that was Robbins, and then the other one hit her and took the gun away. He put a second bullet through Robbins' head and then took the car and split."

"Then Hussein is on his own," Sam said.

"Yeah. They got an APB out on the car, with a warning that he is armed and dangerous."

Sam turned back to Danny. "Danny, did he ever say anything that might give you some idea where he would go? He's going to be looking for someplace to lay low, at least for a little while. He may try to leave Orlando, but that's not going to be easy in a stolen car. Any ideas?"

Danny shook his head. "I'm sorry, man," he said. "Most of the stuff he said to me was about how he was going to kill me if I didn't tell him what he wanted to know."

"No problem," Sam said, "I understand. You listen to the doctors and do what they tell you, and we will probably be back with more questions later."

Sam and Garza left the room, then found a quiet spot to stop and talk.

"So," Sam said. "We have a man who is probably a terrorist running loose around the city, armed and ready to kill anyone who gets in his way. He probably has the bleeding sickness stuff with him, so God only knows what he's planning to do. Got any ideas, Mr. Orlando Detective?"

"Who, me? Who you think I am, Sam Prichard? You're the one with the brains, remember—I'm just along for the ride."

"Yeah, keep telling yourself that," Sam said. "I think our best bet at the moment might be to stay close to Kim. She said Beauregard may have gone after Hussein and Robbins, so he might be able to come back and tell us where Hussein is hiding out."

Garza looked at him for a couple of seconds, then shook his head. "I'm telling you, I have got to get me a couple of ghosts."

* * *

Hussein spotted the police car as it turned into traffic ahead of him and eased his foot off the gas pedal. He let a little more distance get between them, then started looking for somewhere to pull off the street. The last thing he needed was for that cop to notice a car that had probably been reported stolen already.

He spotted a drive-in restaurant and put on the turn signal. Pulling into the parking lot, he went around to the back of the building and found an alley, so he followed that out to a side street. He stopped the car just before pulling onto the street and thought about what to do next.

He was angry. He had told them he wouldn't be able to handle the mission with an idiot like Robbins, an idiot who didn't even believe in the mission at all, but nobody would listen. All he had to do was create a distraction, they told him, find some way to keep the police concerned about something other than the real reason he was there. The bleeding sickness had been working perfectly, but now that stupid boy who created it had been taken by the police, he was probably already giving them the cure. He only needed another day, just one more day, but how was he supposed to get it?

He turned to the right and eased his way into a residential neighborhood. The street was lined with houses on both sides, quaint little houses that looked like they had been designed for moderately affluent families. Hussein knew enough about America to realize that one of those houses probably cost more than his father and brothers together could earn in a lifetime back home. It was why he had joined ISIS, and why he continued to give them his loyalty even after they had so many failures.

"This mission is too important," Saeed had said. "The American president, the great buffoon, will be coming to Orlando. He has a resort there, near the Disney World. We already have people in place, but the police must be kept occupied. They must be kept far too busy to worry about useless patrols and looking at the papers of people who are merely working. Do you understand? This is our chance to strike a blow to the heart of America, by getting rid of the foolish man they have chosen to lead them."

Hussein had understood—that was never the issue. He simply didn't understand how he was supposed to keep an entire city's police department busy with only an idiot to help him.

NINETEEN

"What are you thinking?" Beauregard asked rhetorically. Almost everything he said was rhetorical, since most of the time, no one could hear him.

Hussein was deep in thought, sitting in the car where he had hidden it behind an empty house. The "for sale" sign out front indicated that no one was likely to be stopping in, so it seemed like a good place to hide and think. Not for the first time, Beauregard wished he had the ability to hear the thoughts of the living.

Unfortunately, that only worked with Kim, and she wasn't there. He was on his own, and needed to find some way to figure out what this man was up to and get word back to Sam. That part, he figured, would be easy. He could find the hospital again and Kim would be there; once he reconnected with her, she could tell Sam whatever he learned.

The problems came in when he tried to figure out what the fellow was going to do. He wasn't the sort to speak aloud to himself, so whatever was going on in his mind was taking place silently.

Suddenly, Hussein struck the steering wheel. He muttered something in a language Beauregard could not understand, then took a phone out of his pocket. It wasn't like the phones Sam and his family used; it looked like one of the earliest cell phones that Kim had gotten, fifteen or twenty years earlier. It flipped open, and Hussein used his thumb to dial a number.

Apparently, someone answered the call, because Hussein began speaking rapidly into the phone. He talked for several seconds, and then he stopped to listen to whoever was on the other end of the line. Beauregard watched Hussein's face, and saw the unmistakable look of resignation that came across it.

"You've been given orders, my good man," Beauregard said. "And they are orders that you do not want to follow. I know that look, I've seen it before. You have been told to do something that will likely result in your own death."

As far as Beauregard could tell, Hussein did not have the makings of a bomb, so a suicide bombing didn't seem likely. On the other hand, he had a gun and probably a quart of the bleeding sickness formula; the gun had a few bullets left, so it could probably kill three or four people. The spray bottle was potentially even more deadly.

Hussein spoke again, but this time, he was less enthusiastic. He repeated the same words several times, words that sounded like he was agreeing to something, but there was no way Beauregard could tell what it was.

Finally, the call ended and Hussein tossed the phone onto the seat where Beauregard was sitting. He glanced down at it, amused at where it landed, then immediately put it out of his mind. He needed to figure out what Hussein was going to do, but he hadn't the slightest clue how he might accomplish that.

Hussein got out of the car and walked toward the back door of the house. Beauregard followed and watched as he quickly broke the lock and stepped inside. The house was devoid of any furnishings, and the water faucet yielded nothing when Hussein tried to turn it on. He shook his head in disgust and continued looking through the house.

There were a few boxes sitting in the living room of the house, probably items the previous owners or tenants were planning to return for. Hussein squatted down and looked through the boxes, but there was nothing that seemed to catch his attention. There were books and photos, a few CDs and some knickknacks carefully wrapped in newspaper, but none of that seemed to interest the terrorist.

Finished with his browsing, Hussein got up and walked back out the door and to the car again. Instead of getting in, however, he walked around to the passenger side and opened the door, then reached in and picked up his phone. He looked at it for another moment, then opened it and dialed a number.

Beauregard was expecting another string of unintelligible foreign words, so he was startled when Hussein said, "Hello, Gaba."

There was something that sounded like an excited laugh from the other end of the line, but that was all Beauregard could make out. Hussein listened for a moment, then said, "I am here on business. You know what kind of business, so we need not speak of it on an open line."

He listened again for a moment, then smiled. "I was hoping you would say that," he said. "I need some kind of assistance, Gaba. I am driving a stolen car, so I have had to hide. I am on Catalpa Lane, near the small lakes. What? Yes, that would be about me. I am a bit surprised they have it on the news programming already, but that is what happened. Why? Because he was a fool."

He went back to listening for several seconds, then nodded his head as if the other person could see him. "Yes, I know where it is. I will meet you there. In the meantime, do not let your people relax their diligence even for a moment. I have an idea how I can keep the police busy for another day, but they must not miss the chance to kill the American president. This is the most important opportunity we have ever had, and we need to do something to reclaim honor for our cause. Striking a blow like this against America will be one of the greatest honors we can have."

Beauregard's eyes were big and round. These people were planning to kill the president? Beauregard was fully aware that things were different from his day, when almost anyone could walk up to the president of the United States, and that the current holder of that office would have exceptional security. He couldn't imagine how they expected to get close enough to make an attempt, but he suddenly realized that this was information Sam would need.

Hussein talked on the phone for a moment longer, then ended the call and put the phone into his pocket. He had broken his own rule about being careful what he said over a cell phone, but he didn't even care anymore. The orders he had been given would mean he was never going to see his father and brothers again, so following any precautionary rules seemed a bit ridiculous.

He looked at the car for a moment, then walked around the house and toward the street. He strode down the sidewalk as if he hadn't a care in the world, completely unaware that a Confederate soldier was walking along beside him.

* * *

Sam had called Indie to let her know her mother was in the hospital, but everything was going to be okay. Considering Beauregard's original warning, that someone in Sam's family was going to be afflicted with the illness, having Kim exposed to it after a treatment had already been found was something of a relief. Indie had called and spoken to her mother, who assured her that the doctors said everything was completely under control.

When she was off the phone, Sam looked at his mother-in-law. "Still no sign?" he asked.

Kim shook her head gravely. "Nothing yet," she said. "I wish I could hear your mom, but it doesn't seem to work that way."

Sam nodded, deep in thought. "Kim, has Beauregard ever been away this long before?"

She shook her head, her face blank. "Sam, until just recently, he never got away from me at all. He was always there, and I could always sense him there. Now, I can sometimes go hours without feeling his presence."

Sam scowled. "Now, wait," he said. "I can remember times you said he was off doing his own thing, or something like that."

"Yes, there were times when he was quiet, and even some times when it was almost like I was alone, but there was always that little bit of—well, of *Beauregard* hovering in the background somewhere. I always knew he was there, even when I wasn't sure where he was. And yes, you don't have to say it, I know that makes no sense. It's just how it was, I don't how else to describe it."

Sam bit his tongue. It wasn't her fault the old spook had gone off on a tangent, but it was lousy timing. With any luck, Beauregard might at least have had one of his premonitions. Sam would take anything he could get when there was an armed terrorist running loose.

Garza had called in everything they knew, but that wasn't much. Danny had provided a description of Hussein, but they were still waiting for the police artist to get there and work with him to compose a sketch. They had tried to find any record of his phone, but that was also a dead end. It was undoubtedly a burner phone, anyway, one that could be thrown away at any time.

On the other hand, Sam thought suddenly, there was somebody who was capable of working wonders when it came to electronics. He walked off down the hall to find a quiet spot, then took out his phone to call Indie again.

"Hey, Sam," she said. "Any news?"

"Nothing to write home about," Sam said. "We've run into some dead ends, so I thought I'd ask you if Herman might pull another miracle out of his bag of tricks."

"We can try," she said. "What have you got in mind?"

"This guy, Hussein," Sam said. "The only thing we really know about him is that he seems to be of Middle Eastern descent, he goes by the name Hussein and he has a cell phone. What I'm wondering is, if I give you the approximate times and locations when we know he made a call, is it possible Herman could pick them out of the thousands of calls that might've taken place around the same time?"

"Wow, that's a tall order," she said. "Let me think for a moment. I'd have to get the GPS coordinates for the location, and if you can narrow it down to a small window of time, that would help. Oh, do we have any idea what language he's speaking?"

"Language? Something from the Middle East, I suppose. Danny said it sounded like Arabic to him, but he doesn't really know what it was."

"Well, Herman has access to all of the cloud language databases. What I can do is set him to look for those calls, then find the backup recordings of them. They all get recorded and stored for a period of time, in case the government ever wants to go back and find something you said to use against you. The idea is that he can listen in to a few words, then check the language databases to see if he's got something that came from that area, the Middle East. If he comes up with some that seem to fit, then we can check those against other times and see if the same voices come up. Give me about ten minutes to set up the parameters, and I'll call you right back."

"Okay, babe," Sam said. "I'll go talk to Danny and see about getting all the information I can about those calls."

He put the phone back in his pocket and went down the hall to where Danny was still lying back on the hospital gurney. The young man looked up and smiled when he saw Sam in the room again.

"Danny, you said Hussein made some phone calls. Can you tell me about where you were when he made them, and approximately what time it was?"

"Well, let me think," Danny said. "As a matter of fact, he made a couple of calls yesterday, right after they got me in their van. That was about a quarter after one. I know it was about twenty minutes after I talked to Steve on the Internet, and then they showed up at my apartment and started threatening me. As soon as we got out to the van, Hussein sat in the back with me while Steve drove, and he took out his phone and made a call. He talked for about a minute or so, then he made another one right away. I think that one lasted about a minute, as well." He closed his eyes and thought. "The next time was probably about two hours later, and we were right in front of the main public library. I know because I saw the building through the windshield." He thought a moment longer, then shook his head. "I know there were a couple more calls, but I can't remember exactly when or where. Most of the time I was down on the floor of the van and couldn't really see out."

Sam scribbled down notes on what he had heard. "No, this is good, Danny," he said. "I've got your address, so that first couple of calls had to have been fairly close to there, right?"

"Well, yeah, right outside. Steve had to wait for the trash truck to get out of the way before he could leave my parking lot. It had us blocked in, I just remembered that. Those first two calls had to have happened while we were still sitting there in the parking lot."

Sam grinned. "That's even better," he said. "I'll be back, you just keep resting."

True to her word, Indie called Sam back almost exactly ten minutes later. He quickly read off the information Danny had given him, and she looked at the GPS coordinates for Danny's apartment building.

"Okay, we might get something," she said. "All cell phones now report their GPS locations, even if you think you've got it turned off. That only keeps the average person from getting the information, but the police or the Feds can still pull it up. Let me turn Herman loose, and—there he goes. He'll check every call between one and one thirty that originated from within half a mile of that location. Any of them that come up with a Middle Eastern language will be possible candidates, so then we'll take a look at the GPS history for those phones. When we find the one that has been somewhere we know Hussein has been, we will have his number."

Sam shook his head, grinning into his phone. "Have I ever mentioned how lucky I am that you were homeless that day?"

"Yeah, maybe once or twice," she said, "but I think you were just trying to be flirtatious at the time. You could try telling me again when you get home, and make me really believe it."

Sam chuckled. "You can count on it, babe," he said. "Let me know if you get anything."

"I will, but we could be talking about thousands of phone calls. Even Herman has to spend at least a few seconds listening to each one to figure out what language is being spoken. I would be pretty surprised if we get results anytime soon."

"Well, let me know anyway. Nobody else is going to be able to come close to what you and Herman can do."

They said goodbye and Sam wandered back toward the room where Kim was waiting. Garza was standing outside the door, and he looked excited when he spotted Sam. He hurried in Sam's direction and they met halfway, in the hallway.

"What's up?" Sam asked.

"Maybe a break," Garza said. "A lady on Catalpa Lane, residential area, said she saw a car pull into the driveway of a house that's for sale. A few minutes later, the guy driving the car, who she described as looking like he might be from Iraq or somewhere like that, comes walking out the drive and wanders down the sidewalk. He left the car where it was sitting behind the house, probably because it was out of sight from the street. She waited about ten or fifteen minutes, then called it in."

"How far is that from here?" Sam asked.

"It's a ways," Garza replied. "They already dispatched several cars out there to keep an eye out for the guy, but I just wanted to tell you about it. With any luck, they might be able to pick him up."

"No," Sam said. "This guy may be a bungler, but he's at least something of a professional at what he does. I don't think he is going to be taken without a fight, and since he has already shot a cop and he is definitely armed..."

"Yeah, I know," Garza said. "Suicide by cop, right?"

"I think that's the most likely scenario," Sam said. "And as much as I hate to say it, at least it would put a stop to him."

TWENTY

Hussein had walked nearly a mile, staying off any of the main streets where he might be spotted by police. Beauregard was still beside him, but the man had not spoken again.

"If you would tell me where you are going," Beauregard said, fully aware that he would be ignored since he could not be heard, "then I could hurry back to Samuel and he could arrange a surprise to be waiting for you. But of course, that would require you to be more cooperative than you have been, and that is probably more than I dare hope for."

Of course, Hussein kept walking without saying a word. Beauregard kept pace with him, occasionally speaking only to hear his own voice out of boredom.

They came to a crossing on a major street, and Hussein approached it cautiously. There was no sign of police anywhere in sight, so he hurried across at the light and then turned to the north. A few buildings up, there was a shopping center, and he entered the parking lot as he got closer.

Beauregard was expecting him to try again to steal a car, but Hussein had other things in mind. He walked up to the door of a small convenience store, one that had markings Beauregard suspected were either Arabic or Hindu in origin. Hussein looked through the glass doors, but did not enter. Instead, he smiled and then turned and walked across the front of the building until he got past the windows. He stood there, obviously trying not to be noticed, until a graying, short man came out of the store, carrying a bag. The man walked past Hussein and paid him no attention at all, but Hussein began to follow him. When they got to a large, green pickup truck that was parked in front of an entirely different store, the man looked at Hussein and said, "Get in."

Beauregard slipped into the back seat of the truck and realized that this must be the man Hussein had called earlier. Neither of them spoke until the vehicle was started and backing out of its parking space, and then Hussein looked at the older man.

"Thank you for coming," he said. "I was beginning to wonder what I was going to do."

"I spoke with Hashmi," the older fellow said. "He tells me you have been given a great assignment."

Hussein's face almost betrayed him, but he caught it in time to plaster a smile across it.

"Indeed," he said. "Tomorrow, I shall be in paradise. And you shall be jealous."

"Jealous? Me? Only of the honor that you will receive. You will be a hero, Hussein, a true hero."

"That may be true," Hussein said, "but only if I can find the things I need. Hashmi insists that we make a great impression on the Americans, even with the diversions. I need to make my final mission truly count."

"Have you decided what you're going to do?" the older man asked. "Have you chosen a target?"

"I know of only one place where I can truly be effective at creating the kind of diversion we need," Hussein replied. "The Americans enjoy their vacations, do they not? I will deliver my mission in the midst of them, at Disney World."

The older man nodded. "I suspected you might think of that," he said. "You don't want explosives, then. They have equipment at their gates that can detect them. You will need another way to make your display. Have you thought of anything yet?"

Hussein reached into the side pocket of his cargo pants and retrieved the spray bottle. "This is the bleeding sickness," he said. "This is highly concentrated, so it could easily contaminate many gallons of water. I plan to carry it into the resort, and then look for one of the concession stands that offers bottled water. You see, I was able to send the formula back to Hashmi, and he spoke to someone at the university back home. They confirmed what it could do, but they also found that it could be even more deadly if it is ingested. I plan to take over one of the concession stands. A few drops of this in each bottle, Gaba, and some of the people will begin dying before they even know what is happening."

Gaba looked at the bottle. "On the news programming, they say that the doctors have found a cure. They say that no one else will die because of the bleeding sickness."

"As far as I know, that is true," Hussein replied. "The difference is that, so far, they have only had to deal with those who were infected by touch. When it is swallowed, the damage begins in the throat and the stomach. People will be in agony within minutes, terrible pain, but it will not be connected to the bleeding sickness at first. I think that if dozens of people are dying at the most famous resort in their country, the Americans will find that sufficiently distracting. The police will be searching for me, no doubt, but that will leave fewer officers to interfere with your plans."

The older man looked at Hussein, and there was a bright glimmer of appreciation in his eyes. "I'm certain you are correct," he said. "They go to great lengths to protect that place. I am sure the police will be much more concerned about what is happening to their tourists than they will be about what might happen to the fool they elected as president."

"Indeed," Hussein said. "I will go to Disney World tomorrow morning at ten. Their president is due to arrive at his private resort at eleven, is that correct?"

"Yes," the older man said. "His airplane will land at the Orlando airport, and they have a helicopter waiting there to bring him to the resort. My team will be waiting in the foliage, invisible to their so-called security men. When we open fire, it will happen so fast that they won't have time to react. Not one of them will be left untouched, and they will all be shredded. There will not even be enough left of the president to show at his funeral."

"Then, by noon tomorrow," Hussein said, "we will both be heroes. Let us eat well tonight, my friend. We must celebrate."

Just behind them, unseen by their mortal eyes, the face of Henry Thomas Beauregard twisted in rage.

* * *

Indie and Kenzie had been sitting in the living room together, and Indie was helping her daughter learn one of the new, educational computer games she had bought. While Kenzie was doing well in public school, Indie and Sam both felt that some extra education couldn't hurt. With some of the games that were available, the child was reading and doing math problems that were at least three years ahead of her grade in school.

Herman chimed, and Kenzie looked up at her mother. "Herman, Mom," she said.

"Yes, it was," Indie said. "I better go check and see what he's found."

She got up from the couch and went to the dining room, where she usually used her computer. Sure enough, Herman had several links displayed on the monitor, and each of them had a cell phone number attached to it.

One number was repeated several times, and she clicked on links to see what locations calls had been made from. When she saw that one of the calls was made from the very place where her mother had been abducted, and at about the same time, she realized she had found the one she was looking for.

"Okay, Sam," she said, speaking more to herself. "Get ready for a surprise." She picked up her cell phone and dialed Sam's number, and he answered on the first ring.

"Hey, babe," he said. "Got anything for me?"

"Have I ever," she said. "How would you like Mr. Hussein's phone number? I'm pretty sure I've got it, Sam."

"Okay, how did that happen? I mean, I know Herman is good, but is he really that good?"

"Sometimes I think he's even better than I designed him to be," she replied. "In this case, though, it was just a matter of good programming. He tagged a number that made calls from near Danny's apartment building between one and one thirty yesterday afternoon, and then he kept checking other calls from that number. I have a whole list of them on the screen, but the one that really got my attention was the one that said the phone was used at about the same time my mother was being dragged into that car. Now, I'm not much of a gambler, I admit, but I would bet quite a lot of money that this is the guy we're looking for."

"And I wouldn't bet against you to save my life," Sam said. "Any chance you can figure out where that phone is now?"

"I thought you would never ask," she said sweetly. "Herman is actually giving me live GPS coordinates, updated every few seconds. At the moment, that phone is headed north on South Orange Avenue. It just passed West Michigan Street, so give me another moment…"

He could hear her fingers on the keys of the computer, and Sam couldn't help but grin. The girl he had rescued at the Taco Bell that day had claimed to be good with a computer, but Sam had been amazed when he realized just how proficient she really was. That girl, however, was a rank amateur compared to the current skills Indie had perfected. Even now, after Sam had announced his retirement, she was occasionally called upon by government agencies when they needed someone with her particular abilities.

Of course, what that really meant was that they needed Herman, but he was fickle. For some reason, he wouldn't work properly for anyone else.

"Well, I can tell you that Mr. Hussein, assuming he still has that phone and didn't give it away, is in a green Ford F-150," she said. "That was the only northbound vehicle that went straight at the light on Kaley Street, so that has to be him."

Sam turned quickly to Garza. "Hussein is in a green Ford F-150," he said. "He just passed Kaley Avenue headed north on Orange Avenue. Any chance you've got officers out that way that could do an intercept?"

"There had better be," Garza said. He took out his phone and stepped away so he could call it in.

"Indie, you never cease to amaze me," Sam said. "You may have just brought down a terrorist."

"Hey, don't forget to give credit where credit is due," she said. "Herman did most of the work, I just told him what to look for."

"Then I will be sure to mention Herman when I tell the newspapers who to thank," Sam said, grinning.

"Oh, Sam, you wouldn't," Indie said. "We don't need that kind of publicity, come on."

"I'm teasing you, baby," he said. "I'll tell the police chief, but I'll have him keep that under his hat. No, wait, on second thought, I think maybe we'd better not tell anybody. If we do, somebody down here is going to be calling you constantly. We get enough of that out of Washington already."

"Oh, and speaking of Washington," Indie said, "you will not believe who just showed up at our front door."

Sam grinned. "Would the initials H. W. happen to fit?"

"You knew they were coming? Sam, you should've told me. I could've at least cleaned the house up a little bit."

"I'm sure the house looks just fine, honey. You go on and entertain our guests, and hopefully I'll be able to come home sometime soon. Tell them if they leave before I get there, I'll be mad."

He hung up the phone and went off in search of Garza, who told him that every squad car in that part of the city was on the lookout for that green truck. With any luck, Hussein would soon be stopped from doing any further damage to the city. Sam was just about to let himself hope for a quick end to the problem when everything suddenly went crazy.

"*SAM!*"

Sam turned instantly and hurried toward Kim's room, because it was her voice that screamed out his name so loudly. He got to the room and found her on her feet, arguing with a nurse who was trying to get her to get back on the bed before she ripped the IV line out of her arm.

"Kim? What's going on?"

Kim tried to speak, but suddenly her eyes glazed over and the nurse had to catch her to keep her from falling. A second later, she managed to get her balance and looked at Sam.

The difference in her face was obvious, and Sam knew that he was about to be speaking with Beauregard again.

"Samuel," Beauregard said, "things are much more dire than I first believed. I have been with the murderous bastard who has been behind these heinous crimes, and he is preparing to sink even lower."

"Beauregard, what are you talking about?" Sam asked. "What's going on?"

"Sam, that man is not alone. There are more of his group in the city, and the majority of them are planning to strike at the president when he arrives tomorrow. Mr. Hussein is to create a diversion, and he's come up with a diabolical plan to do so. He intends to take the liquid that causes the bleeding sickness and put it into water bottles, which will be given out at the Disney World park, where you took your children."

Sam looked confused. "Okay, that's bad, but at least we know how to treat it, now," he said, but Kim was shaking her head.

"Samuel," Beauregard's voice said, still coming from Kim's lips, "that was when it was absorbed through the skin. According to Mr. Hussein, it is far more deadly when consumed by mouth."

Sam stared at Kim for another moment, then turned and bolted out of the room once again. He hurried down the hall to Danny's room and rushed inside.

"Danny, tell me, quickly. What would happen if someone were to drink the liquid they used to infect the money?"

"Drink it? Good Lord, I don't think anybody could. The stuff smells horrible, and…"

"What if it were diluted in bottles of water? Would that make a difference?"

Denny stared at him for a couple of seconds, then slowly nodded. "It would make a hell of a difference," he said. "For one thing, the stuff could be diluted almost two hundred to one with water, and it would still be potent enough to eat the esophageal and stomach linings. Oh, I can't believe I didn't think of that. Mr. Prichard, it would be twice as deadly that way, maybe even worse than that. People would be choking on their own blood within twenty, maybe thirty minutes at most."

"What about treatment? Would the same medicine you're using still help?"

Denny shook his head. "I'm sorry, no. By the time it was swallowed, the damage would already have started, and I don't think anything could stop it fast enough to save the victim. There wouldn't be anything the doctors could do, Mr. Prichard."

Sam turned and left the room again, hurrying down the hall in search of Doctor Dione, but one of the nurses told him that she was sleeping. She had been on her feet for more than forty hours straight, and had been forced to go and lie down for a while.

Sam went back to Garza. "Any luck on finding that truck?" he asked.

Garza shook his head. "No," he said. "It seems to have disappeared. They've even been scanning the traffic cameras, but there's no sign of it anywhere."

Turning away for a moment, Sam took out his phone and hit the speed dial icon for Indie.

"Indie, we lost Hussein," Sam said. "Are you still tracking his phone?"

"Just a second," she said. "Let me get to the computer. Come on, Herman, where is he? Oh, Sam, I'm sorry, he must have figured the phone might lead us to him. The signal is gone, he probably took out the battery."

"Okay," Sam said. "Keep trying, just in case he turned it back on. If anything comes up, call me instantly. This thing just got worse than ever."

"Sam? What do you mean, worse than ever?"

Sam took a deep breath. "Apparently, Hussein is planning to put the poison into water bottles and take them to Disney World to give out. It seems the effects are far more deadly that way, and there won't be any way to save anyone who drinks it. He's only supposed to be creating a diversion so that another cell can try to attack the president when he arrives tomorrow. If we suddenly have hundreds of people, including kids, getting sick at a place like Disney—well, that would be one heck of a diversion."

"Oh my God, Sam," Indie said softly. "I'll keep looking. Maybe Herman can find something connected to him to zero in on."

The line went dead and Sam bit his bottom lip, doing his best not to tremble with rage. The very thought of someone taking a poison that deadly into such a happy place, potentially giving it to children like his own daughter and little boy, was enough to make him want to disembowel the man who was sadistic enough to do it.

"Okay," he said after a moment. "The first thing we need to do is get word to the chief about the planned attempt on the president. They need to start looking for anyone who might be in a position to get close to him that hasn't been properly vetted, and they need to move fast. As for Hussein, he's planning to hit Disney World tomorrow. You and I and a whole bunch more are going to be waiting for him."

TWENTY-ONE

The doctor on duty agreed to release Kim about a half hour later—after giving her three different bottles of medication to take home—and Garza drove her and Sam back to the police station, so that Sam could pick up his car. The two men talked for a few moments on the way, finalizing the plan for the following morning.

Beauregard had told them that Hussein was planning to be at Disney World by ten, so Garza had arranged for a large number of officers, many of whom were giving up their day off, to be wandering around the park pretending to be tourists. Under the circumstances, Disney's security had agreed to cooperate, something they genuinely seemed to hate doing. The alternative, however, could mean they would have a number of dead guests, and that would certainly be bad for business.

Sam promised to meet Garza at seven, and it was already established that Kim would be coming along. Beauregard would be the only witness they had who could actually recognize Hussein on sight, but they also had the sketch that had finally gotten done. The sketch artist had arrived late, but at least he had shown up.

The ride home was fairly quiet, with Kim contemplating how close she had come to death. They were almost back to Flagler Beach when she finally looked over at Sam.

"How did you do it?" she asked.

"I beg your pardon?"

"Don't play dumb, Sam. I want to know how you did it, how you got up every day and went out and did your job knowing that almost any one of those days could be your last. Today was the closest I have come to dying in a long time, maybe in forever. I know, we've been through some things before, but this time it really hit home. I mean, those guys were going to kill us. They had every intention of taking us somewhere and killing us, and we wouldn't even have gotten to say goodbye to our families, or—or anything. I don't know how you did it, I really don't."

She turned and looked out the windshield again. Sam chewed on his bottom lip for a moment, then said, "I guess I did it because somebody has to."

Kim didn't say a word the rest of the way home, but when they pulled into the driveway and Sam shut off the car, she reached over and put a hand on his arm.

"You're right," she said. "Somebody has to. And tomorrow morning, I'll go with you again. You'll need Beauregard, but that means you have to be stuck with me, as well."

She turned without another word and got out of the car while Sam did the same. He let her precede him onto the porch and felt himself smile when Indie, holding Bo, and Kenzie came running to greet her. Kim got all the attention for a few minutes, but that was okay with Sam. He'd had that attention a few times himself, and sometimes it was exactly what you needed.

"About time, Sam, boy," Harry said. He and his wife were sitting on the sofa, and Harry was holding an unlit cigar. He started pulling himself forward, his age catching up with him as he struggled a bit to get up off of the couch. "You, me, the front porch. This cigar and I have been waiting several hours for you to get here, and that's just too long."

Sam chuckled and turned back to the door, leading the way out onto the porch where a couple of chairs and the small table awaited them. While Sam personally didn't mind Harry's cigars, Indie found them a bit too potent. Cigar smoking, she decreed, was to take place on the front porch or back deck, but nowhere inside the house.

"So," Harry said. "I gather you have saved the day once again?"

"Not exactly," Sam said. He told Harry everything that had happened during the day, and about the planned attempt on the president the following day. He expected Harry to be pretty upset about that, but the old man simply took another puff on the cigar and nodded.

"You're not worried about an assassination attempt on the president?" Sam asked.

"Not particularly," Harry said. "He's got an incredibly good protection detail, Sam, and I know because I trained a few of them. As a matter of fact, I think I trained the people who trained the rest of them, so I know they're good. I learned a long time ago that the best way to be an instructor was to make sure your students turned out better than you were."

Sam grinned. "Okay, I get your point. Anyway, Detective Garza has lined up a lot of officers, both male and female, who will be playing tourist at Disney World tomorrow morning. I'm going to be there as well, along with Kim. She has to come along because…"

"I know," Harry said. "When I saw that she was with you today, it didn't take too many of my few remaining brain cells to figure out that Beauregard was lending you a hand. How is that working out for you, by the way? Indie has filled me in a little bit, and I'd like to hear it from you."

Sam looked at him suspiciously. "If I answer you," he said, "am I suddenly going to find federal agents showing up in my house to ask the ghost for help?"

"Not from telling me," Harry said. "Half the stuffed shirts in Washington already think I'm crazy; do you think I'm going to mention the Civil War ghost who helps out my buddy Sam? They'd have me in Bellevue before you could buy me a get-well card."

Sam grinned. "Okay, then," he said. "Lately, Beauregard has been a lot more mobile than he used to be. He says he doesn't know why, but he can move away from Kim, now, ever since my mother ended up joining him. They helped out a lot on this case, because they were able to interview some of the victims."

"Wait, what did you say? They were able to interview the victims?"

Sam nodded, grinning again. "That's what I said," he said. "Harry, the victims of this thing were unconscious from the moment it hit them until the moment they died. The only way to get any information out of them was to let Beauregard and Mom talk to them once they stopped breathing."

For the first time in Sam's long association with Harry Winslow, the old man was actually speechless. His mouth was hanging open as he stared at Sam, and Sam was starting to wonder if hearing about their ghostly exploits had been too much for him.

A moment later, Harry closed his mouth. "Sam," he said, "if anyone else told me the story I just heard come out of your mouth, I would have said he was either an incredibly imaginative liar, or completely out of his mind. Having met Beauregard, however, I am forced to conclude that you were telling me the exact truth. Do you have any idea what I would have given for an agent who could interview the dead?"

"Harry, don't you dare mention a word of this to anyone," Sam said. "I've already got Garza talking about how he needs to find a couple of ghosts. I don't want to hear it out of you, as well."

"I'm not going to say anything. Good Lord, Sam, boy, I do like what little freedom I got left, you know?" He grinned suddenly. "On the other hand, have you thought about the possible commercial implications?"

"Commercial? I don't follow, Harry."

"Why, Sam, just think about all the people who didn't get to tell their loved ones something important before they died. Your ghosts could probably hang out at hospitals and rack up some healthy rewards for delivering important final messages."

Sam stared at Harry for a moment. "If you so much as mention that to Kim, I will personally kick your ass," he said.

Harry chuckled. "You think that might offend her, do you?"

"That's the problem, Harry," Sam said. "I don't know if it would offend her, or give her ideas. And to be honest, I really don't want to find out."

The two of them entertained each other while Harry smoked a cigar, and then they wandered back into the house. The adults ended up playing cards for a while after the children were put to bed, and then Sam announced that he needed to get some sleep to be ready for the next morning.

"Well, you're going to have some company," Harry said. "Kathy and I have decided we need to visit Disney World. I figure there's bound to be something an old fart like me can do for fun there, right?"

"Harry, that's not necessary," Sam said. "We've got plenty of people who will be on station."

"No sense trying, Sam," Kathy said. "I think he's just as bored as you were. If we don't let him go along and try to help catch one more bad guy, I will never hear the end of it."

Sam rolled his eyes, then shrugged and grinned. "Okay," he said. "In that case, the guest room is right down the hall. You'd better get some sleep, yourselves. I'm getting up at five, because I've got to be at the Orlando PD at seven."

They all said good night, and Sam and Indie retired to their bedroom. They quickly got ready for bed and climbed in, cuddling up together as they drifted off to sleep.

Morning came much earlier than Sam wanted it to, but the sun peeking over the edge of the world meant it was time for him to get up. He eased himself out of bed so that he wouldn't wake Indie, then took a quick shower, shaving while he was at it. He came out of the bathroom wearing a towel, then dropped it on the floor as he started climbing into his clothes.

Just like the day before, he found Kim sitting in the kitchen with a pot of coffee already made. He thanked her and got himself a cup, and then the two of them left the house and headed for Orlando.

They met up with Garza as planned, then started preparing for the day's operation. More than two dozen officers, most of whom were supposed to be off for the day, had volunteered to participate. There were also three agents from the FBI field office and quite a few from the sheriff's office. Altogether, Sam and Garza were put in command of more than forty law enforcement officers.

Garza had run off copies of the sketch and was passing them out while Sam briefed them all about the scant details they had about Mr. Hussein.

"We don't really know much about him," Sam said. "He seems to be from someplace where Arabic is a common language, and he is quite violent. He's more than willing to kill anyone he thinks is in his way, and we can expect him to be armed. You're all getting a copy of the sketch we have of him, but we also have one eyewitness who has personally seen him." He introduced Kim, briefly touching on the fact that she was abducted, along with Emma and Danny. "She'll be staying pretty close to me, but she'll be keeping her eyes peeled so that we have the best chance of catching this guy before he can do any harm."

There were a few questions and Sam answered them as quickly and efficiently as he could, and then they all started heading for the door. They were all going to the park in their personal vehicles, to avoid a sudden confluence of police cars showing up in the parking areas. When Sam and Kim came out to get in the Mustang, he noted with approval that they were staggering their departures. That way, they wouldn't all be showing up at the same time. While there might be a lot of vehicles arriving every minute, the drivers probably did not know one another. It was entirely possible that Hussein would be smart enough to spot it if a bunch of men and women climbed out of different cars, but seemed to know one another well. That would indicate there was something secretive about their presence, and would probably lead to the conclusion that they were some sort of undercover police officers.

Meanwhile, another whole section of the police department was working with the Secret Service and FBI to protect the president. Because Hussein was known to have been involved in the bleeding sickness attack, the intelligence that indicated danger to the president was taken seriously.

Sam was relieved. While he trusted Harry's confidence in the president's security team, he also knew from experience that it was easy to be blindsided. The more effort they put into protecting the president, the more confident Sam would be that they would get the job done.

* * *

Beauregard and Grace walked along beside Sam and Kim as they made their way toward the monorail. Parking at Disney World meant something entirely different than anywhere else, because you would end up riding a tram from the parking lot to the monorail station, and then the monorail would take you to the entrance of the park.

"Goodness," Grace said, "I'm just as excited about coming here as I was when I was alive."

Beauregard looked at her with one eyebrow raised. "I confess I have never seen the excitement in places like this," he said. "Of course, I have only heard of them and seen them on Miss Kimberly's television, until recently. Our visit here in the springtime was my first actual experience with such a place."

"You've got to be kidding," Grace said. "How can you not love Disney World? How can anybody not love Disney World? There's so much to do. I mean, you can go on the rides and, and there's lots of things to see. Oh, personally, I always loved the Carousel of Time. We have to watch that, if we have time."

Beauregard heaved another sigh, but there was a glint of happiness in his eye. Grace had certainly become an important part of his existence, and he found himself enjoying the entertainment she provided.

It was nine a.m., and most of the officers working with them were already inside the park. Sam and Kim stepped up to the window and Sam bought their tickets for the day, and then they wandered inside. They had decided to stay close to the front entrance, to give both Beauregard and Kim the best chance to spot Hussein as he entered the park.

Because Grace had also seen Hussein, the two ghosts decided they could help cover more ground by splitting up. Since Beauregard had been able to leave Grace's presence before, he had concluded that it was probably safe to do so. After a quick conference with Kim and Sam, they stationed themselves at different spots where they could watch the entrances.

Grace, who was actually finding the afterlife to be a lot of fun, picked a spot where she could see well, but also watch some of the people around her. She sat down on air and folded her legs under herself, prepared to wait for hours if necessary. That's probably why she was so startled when a boy of about ten years old walked up to her and cocked his head to the side.

"What are you sitting on?" he asked.

Grace looked at him, and he returned her gaze. "You can see me?" she asked.

"Well, yeah," the kid said. "I just can't see what you're sitting on."

Grace looked down. "Oh," she said. She unfolded her legs and stood up. "How long have you been here?" she asked him.

"I don't know," he said. "A while, now. It's a fun place to hang out."

Grace bit her bottom lip for a moment, then leaned down and looked him in the eye. "Do you understand what's going on?"

The kid looked at her askance. "What do you mean?"

"Oh, you poor thing," Grace said. "I mean, do you understand what happened to you?"

"What happened to me? What are you talking about, lady?"

"Well…" Grace stuttered. "You can see me. Aren't you—I mean, aren't you—aren't you dead?"

The kid tilted his head and looked at her like she had grown a third eye. "Dead? Lady, you're weird." He shook his head and turned to walk away. Grace stared after him, tempted to try to run after him and get to know him better, but she spotted Beauregard watching her. She frowned and turned to watch the entrance again.

An hour passed with no sign of Hussein, and Sam began to wonder if he had changed his mind and chosen another target. He said as much to Kim, but she shook her head.

"Beauregard says he's coming," she said. "He'll be here soon, but we might not recognize him."

Sam scowled and rolled his eyes. "There he goes again," he said. "Vague predictions. It'd be nice if he could tell us why we won't recognize him."

Kim shrugged. "If he could, he would, Sam. It's not his fault he doesn't get all the details."

"I know, I know. The thing is, if we don't spot this guy, people could die. I don't want that on my conscience, Kim."

"Neither do I, Sam. All we can do is keep watching."

Sam turned his eyes to the entrance again and carefully studied everyone who came through the gates. There had to be something that would give Hussein away, no matter how he might have disguised himself. And how could he really disguise himself, anyway? From the sketch, it looked to Sam like the best he would be able to do might be to change his hair color and put on a pair of glasses.

"What about that guy?" Kim asked, pointing at a man who had just come through the gate. "That looks a little like him."

Sam looked closely. "Are you sure?"

"Well, I'm not sure," Kim said. "Beauregard? What do you think? Could that be him?" She looked at an empty space for a moment, then turned back to Sam. "That's not him," she said.

Sam let out a breath in frustration. How could he possibly know Hussein if he saw him, considering the best he had was a sketch? If Kim wasn't confident of recognizing him, there wasn't much hope for the rest of them.

A couple of kids let out a shout across the courtyard, and Sam automatically glanced over to see what caught their attention. An actor dressed as Goofy had just come through the gates with a bag slung over his shoulder, and children were rushing toward him.

Sam turned back to the gates, but something suddenly didn't feel right. He looked around the courtyard again, half convinced that Hussein was already there and laughing at them as they tried to spot him. He turned once more toward the gates, but then the children gave another shout and he glanced involuntarily back at Goofy.

Goofy was reaching into his bag, and a sudden block of ice hit

Sam in the gut. He started toward the children and the actor without even thinking, but then he was moving as fast as his limp would allow.

Beauregard saw Sam moving and looked ahead of him. There was somebody dressed in some sort of dog costume, surrounded by children, but that was all he saw. He didn't know why Sam was hurrying toward them, but he knew how reliable Sam's instincts could be. He looked more closely at the man in the costume, and then realized what was happening.

Goofy had pulled out bottles of water and was holding them up over his head while the children were jumping up and down and calling for him to give them away. He remembered Hussein talking about mixing the poison into water bottles for the people at this place, and felt a chill of his own.

Grace was closest to the man in the costume, but there wasn't much she could do. Beauregard launched himself into the air, shouting for Grace at the same time.

Grace turned and saw Goofy holding out bottles of water, and then she saw the little boy who had spoken to her in the throng around him. Something inside her boiled over into a rage, and she left the ground instantly, crossing the distance to the costumed man in only seconds. Instinctively, she reached out to grab hold of him, but her hands passed right through his back, and then the world went into slow motion.

She saw Sam trying to hurry toward them, and Goofy was bringing down the bottles of water, two in each hand, that he was about to pass out to the children. Without even thinking about what she was doing, Grace surged forward and passed right through Goofy. The rage she was feeling inside boiled over and she let out a scream, and then everything went back to normal.

Grace saw the faces of almost a dozen children, all staring at her.

She glanced down at herself and realized that she was actually leaning through the actor's body, and even though Disney World is a place of magic, these children weren't entirely sure what they were seeing.

One of them lost interest and reached for the bottle of water Goofy was holding, and Grace snapped out of her surprised reverie.

"No," she said, "you don't want that!"

The child, a girl of about ten or eleven years old, caught hold of the water bottle. Goofy held on to it for a moment, playing with her, keeping her attention focused on the bottle, and Grace finally lost it completely. She reared back and let out the loudest scream she could, leaning down into the faces of the children who somehow could see her, and making herself as frightening as she possibly could.

It worked. The girl who had gotten the first water bottle dropped it suddenly and turned to run, while all the other children scattered screaming in different directions. Grace spun around and tried to rip the mask off the actor, but once again, her hands only passed through him.

And then she noticed that he was frozen, standing perfectly still. His eyes, big and round, seemed to be locked on hers, and she realized that, somehow, he could see her just as the children had been able to.

"You're a monster," she hissed. "Only a monster would harm children."

Hussein stumbled backward, his eyes locked on the somehow transparent face that was scowling at him, and the visage was so terrible that he screamed just as the children had done. His eyes were wide and his hands were out in front of him, as if he was trying to push something away.

Sam, running toward the man in the Goofy costume, suddenly saw him stumble backward and begin screaming. He blinked, trying to figure out why his prey suddenly looked blurry, but then he realized some sort of mist in the air was distorting his view. He shook his head to clear it and then dived through the mist, tackled Goofy and took him to the ground, while other law enforcement officers were running in their direction. Beauregard caught up at that moment, and put a protective arm around Grace to pull her aside while Sam cuffed the man in the furry suit.

Sam pulled the mask off, and Beauregard and Grace both felt a sense of relief. The man in the suit was Hussein, and his plans were foiled.

Kim arrived then, and told Sam that he definitely had the right man. Sam grinned and handed Hussein off to two of the FBI agents, who had come running when they saw Sam moving so quickly. The agents took him away, and Sam turned to Kim.

"I just saw something really strange," he said. "He was passing out water to the children, or he was about to. He was holding it over his head, like he was playing keep-away, but the kids were reaching forward and he started to hand it to them—and then all of a sudden, the kids started screaming and ran away. I mean they were screaming, like terrified screaming, and then—well, then it seemed like there was something between me and him, something—well, something ghostly, I guess." He looked around to make sure no one else was within earshot. "Is Beauregard here? Did he do something that scared the children off?"

Kim started to speak, but then she stopped and listened. A moment later, she started laughing.

"Oh, Sam," she said. "That wasn't Beauregard that scared the kids. Sam, that was your mother."

Sam's eyes went wide. "Mom? She did that somehow?"

"Yes, Sam," Kim said, still grinning. "Beauregard says it had something to do with her rage. She was so angry that Hussein was trying to poison those children that she actually became visible for a moment. That was her you saw, Sam, not Beauregard."

EPILOGUE

Sam looked through the one-way glass at the man sitting at the table in the interrogation room. Garza, beside him, let out a sigh.

"The Feds haven't been able to get him to talk at all," he said. "They were about to call in somebody else when they got a phone call that said to let you take a crack at him."

Sam nodded slowly. "I heard," he said. "Let's see if I can get anything out of him." He turned aside and went out into the hall, then entered the interrogation room. Garza and an FBI agent named Morgan were watching through the glass as Sam stepped up to the table and looked down at the man who was handcuffed to it.

"I suppose you feel like you've done something important," Sam said. "You and your buddies didn't manage to accomplish what you set out to do, but I guess that makes you some kind of martyrs, right? You're going to suffer for the cause, is that it?"

Hussein sat there without saying anything, his eyes locked on the surface of the table.

"Mr. Hussein, under the current laws in this country, you can be classified as an enemy combatant. That means you don't have any rights, and you will probably never have any chance at seeing freedom again. You will spend the rest of your life in rooms like this, with people like me trying to get answers out of you. When that fails, they will simply leave you sitting in your cell, with nothing to do and no one to talk to. If there's anything that can drive a man mad more than absolute boredom, I'm not sure I know what it is. You've got a small window of opportunity to get yourself a better deal, and it's not far from closing. If you talk to me now, tell me everything about this particular cell and what their missions are, you can probably get a lighter sentence. Even spending some time in federal prison is better than Guantánamo Bay, wouldn't you think?"

Hussein adjusted himself in the chair, but still didn't reply. Sam decided to try another tack.

"Okay, you don't want to talk, that's fine with me. I really don't mind the idea that you're going to suffer. On the other hand, there is one thing I'm really, really curious about, and it's not something that's going to hurt your friends. Just before I got hold of you, you let out a scream. What was that all about? What did you see that scared you that bad?"

Sitting at the table, Hussein tensed. His hands clenched into fists, then his face contorted into a rictus of fear, but he still said nothing.

"Wow, it's got you scared even now," Sam said. "Must have been pretty frightening, whatever it was. Sure you don't want to talk about it? It might help, you know, make it a little less terrifying."

"You know nothing," Hussein hissed at him. "What I saw—never did I believe in such demons before, but now I have seen with my own eyes."

"Oh, the demon," Sam said. "Let me guess, looked like a woman with dark hair? She was probably really angry, ready to tear you into shreds?"

For a split second, Hussein glanced up at him, but then he put his eyes back on the table. "You have seen the thing before?" he asked.

"Many times," Sam said, chuckling. He sat his right hip on the table and leaned down toward Hussein. "And I can tell you, she's every bit as scary as she looked. Now, you want to know the best part? She's not the only one there is. There's another one, and they both work with me. If you like, I can bring them in and see if you can avoid telling them what we want to know."

Hussein's eyes jerked up at him. "You're lying," he said. "No one can control the demon."

"Well, then why did she come after you that way? You are about to do something terrible, you'd think a demon would have wanted you to go ahead. Demons are evil, right? Just like you?"

"But how could you control it? A demon is not a creature that you can punish or reward."

Sam grinned at him. "Well, then I guess I should let you know my secret," he said. "You see, that demon? She just happens to be my mother."

Hussein's eyes grew wide for a moment, but then they narrowed in suspicion. "That is a lie," he said. "You could not be the child of a demon—that is not possible."

Sam let his grin go a bit wider. "Want me to prove it? Just a minute, let me get her in here."

He got to his feet and started toward the door, but Hussein called out after him. "Wait!"

Sam turned back to face him. "Oh, you ready to talk now?"

Hussein licked his lips and then looked back at the table. "What do you wish to know?"

Sam walked back over and sat down in the chair on the opposite side of the table. He leaned forward and looked at Hussein for a long few seconds, then said, "I want to know who put this mission together. I want to know all the details. Why were you trying to attack the president, and why did you kill all those people?"

Hussein glared at him for a couple of seconds, then looked at the table again. "I told them we should never have taken this mission," he said. "It was foolish, but Hashmi said we needed the money." He took a deep breath, then looked up at Sam once more. "Hashmi is our leader. Gaba is the man who runs the cell here, the one who was orchestrating the attack on your president. I was only supposed to do things to keep your police busy. The idea for the bleeding sickness came from one of your own people, and it won Hashmi's approval. Making the poison was easy and we found someone to do it for us, then I used some American college students who are disillusioned with your country to help me disseminate it. One of them worked for the company that puts money in the dispenser machines, and it proved to be an effective way to spread the poison. That is all I was supposed to do until you figured it out, and then they wanted me to create an even bigger diversion during the attack."

He paused, so Sam filled in the gap. "So you decided to poison a bunch of children?"

"You Americans love your fun times," Hussein said contemptuously. "If you had not stopped me, your police and federal agents would have been too busy looking for me in the Disney park to bother with any extra measures to protect the president. Gaba would have gotten his missile fired and the mission would have been accomplished."

"No, it wouldn't," Sam said. "You see, one of those demons you keep talking about was staying very close to you yesterday. That's how we knew what you were planning to do, and it's also how we knew where to look for Gaba and his people. They were arrested even before we figured out that you were the man in the Goofy costume."

Hussein shrugged. "It doesn't matter anymore," he said. "I told Hashmi that we should not have taken the mission, we could have gotten money some other way. He insisted we accept, though, because they offered so much money. Twenty-five million American dollars, that's how much they paid Hashmi to send us on this mission."

Sam's eyebrows rose. "Twenty-five million? Who paid you?"

Hussein shook his head. "I don't know exactly," he said. "Some of your American businesses, they are displeased with the way your president is doing things. They wanted him removed, because the man who would replace him would be easier to control."

Sam looked at him for a moment. "You're saying that American companies paid to have the president assassinated?"

"Is that not what I said? I only regret that I do not know who they were, because I would gladly share my punishment with them."

"Does Gaba know who they were?" Sam asked.

Hussein shook his head once more. "No," he said. "He knew only that he was given orders. He was told that the president was an obstacle to everything we are trying to do, and that was good enough for him."

Sam got up and walked out of the room, and wasn't surprised to find three FBI agents standing in the hallway.

"I take it you heard?" Sam asked.

Agent Morgan nodded. "We did, Mr. Prichard. That's good work, nobody else has gotten anything out of him."

Sam shrugged. "I just knew which buttons to push," he said. "Considering what we just learned, I suspect that you will be taking over the investigation?"

"We already have it where the terror cell is concerned," Morgan said. "This guy, though, he's basically all yours. The only thing we ask is that any intel you get out of him should be shared with us."

"Absolutely," Sam said. "I'm sure the Orlando Police Department will be more than happy to do so."

"You're not going to stay on the case?"

"My part is done," Sam said. "I was only consulting on this case, so I'm probably going to head for home."

"Not yet, you're not," Morgan said. "I've been told to require you to stay here overnight, so that you can meet with the president in the morning. He wants to know everything about this case, and he'd like you to help strategize about how to find out who was behind this. When we tell him it was American corporations, he's probably going to be livid."

Sam scowled. "I live less than two hours away," he said. "I'm going home tonight, and I'll be back tomorrow morning."

"I'm afraid not, Mr. Prichard," Morgan said. "The president was most insistent that you remain here until you can talk with him tomorrow."

Sam frowned. "Fine, then," he said. "Whatever the president wants, I guess."

He turned and walked down the hall, found an empty office and went in to sit down. He took out his phone to call Indie and let her know what was happening, then put his feet up on the desk and adjusted his hips until he was comfortable.

Sam was treated to a room at the same resort the president was staying in for the night, and then was invited to join him for breakfast the following morning. When he got to the dining area, he was surprised to find Garza and several other people from the police and FBI already there.

"Come in, come in," POTUS said. "Plenty of room, we've got eggs and bacon and grits, all kinds of stuff."

Sam got a cup of coffee and sat down at the table, then helped himself to a plate of eggs and bacon. The chitchat around the table was mundane, mostly about the weather and a couple of sports teams. It wasn't until after breakfast that they were all taken to a conference room.

"What I ask of you gentlemen and ladies," the president said, "is that you do your best to figure out who could have been behind this attack. We know that it's got something to do with big business, and

I have a few suspicions on who might be involved, but I need proof. I'm hoping that all of you can come up with something."

They set to work, and everything was sorted into a timeline kind of order. Unfortunately, nothing any of them had learned had any connection to any particular business, so they were—as Sam put it—at the end of their ropes.

Lunch was brought to them in the conference room that day, so they continued working as they ate. It wasn't until after lunch that they were informed the president had called in some kind of special assistance to help with the investigation.

A few hours later, Sam heard the door open and turned to see who was entering. His jaw dropped when he recognized the man coming through the door, and he was tempted to run out the door.

The conversation with the special investigator didn't last long, and then Hussein was turned over to yet another agency for interrogation. Sam didn't like the tactics that would be used, but he decided not to complain.

And then it was time for him to go home. He left the resort and got into his Mustang, started the big engine and pointed it northeast. Harry Winslow had driven down the day before to pick up Kim, so Sam was able to head directly for home.

As he drove, he thought about his decision to be a consulting detective. While there were still risks involved, he had to admit to himself that it felt good to be back in the saddle. And now that he had the assistance of Beauregard and his mother, Sam had a feeling the cases were going to be even more interesting than they had been in the past.

GET DAVID ARCHER'S STARTER LIBRARY FOR FREE

Sign up for my no-spam newsletter and get two introductory novella's, two introductory audiobook's, and advanced discounted links to new releases, all for free.

Get instant access at www.davidarcherbooks.com/sign-up

ALSO BY DAVID ARCHER

Up to date books can be found on my website:
www.davidarcherbooks.com

NOAH WOLF THRILLERS

SAM PRICHARD MYSTERIES

CHANCE REDDICK THRILLERS